The Princess and the Dragon and Other Stories About Unlikely Heroes

By Francesca Astraea

A couple of people kind-of-jokingly asked me to remember them come dedication time. I'd prefer to come across as sage and ethereal in these fancy centred italics, but firstly I actually remembered and secondly am quite grateful for your time, now I think about it.
Thus: thank you to two very different teachers, Lucy Wilkins and Maggie Stiefvater.

Finally, thank you to everyone who read or encouraged this novel in the months and years it took to grow it from scratchings and a good feeling into the excellent piece of literature you're about to read.
Yeah, I just called my own work excellent.
You're going to have to keep reading now to see if I'm right hahahaaa.

Contents

Prologue

Not all fairy tales have happy endings. Some end with a marriage, which could be a happy ending or a happy beginning, depending on how you look at it. Some end neatly, which could be a happy ending or a sad ending but is more often quite a boring one. Then there is this fairy tale, which ends neither happily nor neatly.

The island of the Three Kingdoms is tucked away at the edge of nowhere and surrounded by violent sea on all sides. It slightly resembles a crescent moon and greatly resembles the sort of place you find silver-tongued elderly ladies with a tendency to cast enchantments and witty young men with a tendency to embark on valiant quests and declare themselves heroes. There are surprisingly high levels of hygiene and health and safety given the lack of electricity and standardised paperwork.

Several thousand years before the witty men and the hygiene standards, the Three Kingdoms was merely a small, volatile, pocket of ocean. One afternoon the earth sneezed, accidentally spewing out a handful of magical creatures, a variety of poisonous plants and four strains of the common cold. The ocean viewed all these things as the unfortunate natural by-product of a sneeze and made to clear them away, so the earth hastily spat out a spectacular island of mountain ranges and beaches and lush green valleys, offering its exiles a comfortable prison. Magic seeped through the earth and out into the sea, calling out for humans to come and look and stay a while. This was probably where things went wrong.

The islanders promptly set about harnessing the magic and taming the creatures and figuring out which plants could be eaten if cooked properly. They also named the Three Kingdoms the Three Kingdoms *of* something, but they kept claiming one another's thrones via wars or marriages (or a war disguised as a marriage) until specifics faded away and all that remained were three royal families and three tenacious nations, mutually enjoying the eternal bonds of shared history and common culture.

Well, three royal families and three tenacious nations with a lot of shared history.

The Princess and
the Dragon

Chapter One

The Kingdom of Mirrors, the loudest, southernmost and most magical of the Three Kingdoms, filled the bottom third of the crescent moon with olive trees, fishing boats and about ten thousand mirrors. It was ruled by the Durante line of the House of Stars, whose family tree was dotted with the types of people whose exploits are written into ten-minute songs about burning cities, eccentric fashion sense and enormous acts of courage in the face of fire-breathing dragons. Princess Amelia, the youngest of the Durante family, knew from early childhood that she, too, would one day have to defeat a dragon.

Nobody initially expected Amelia to face the dragon in question, partly because she was a girl and partly because she had been born second in line to the throne. Her older brother, Prince Nicholas, was both dashingly handsome and perfectly capable of embarking on such a heroic quest by himself. Unfortunately for Amelia, by the time she reached her teens Prince Nicholas found himself indisposed, so although most people were too polite to mention it, the task of dragon-slaying ultimately fell to her.

Amelia was fourteen, and in happier stories she would be learning how to dance or dabble in magic. In this story, Amelia was in charge of olive oil production. She was also kingdom treasurer, head of the royal family's public relations department, occasional fisherwoman and part-time carer to her ailing father, the king. For someone born into a centuries-old dynasty, she spent a lot of time with ancient legal documents and recently gutted fish.

Amelia's path to notoriety began one overwarm Monday evening in early spring when she had finished a day's work in the kingdom treasury and was heading through the Kingdom of Mirrors' busy capital city, Lumiere, to evening lessons in the castle. Today she would be learning mathematics with her tutor—which seemed redundant when she ran the entire kingdom's budget from a piece of parchment and an abacus—so she dragged her feet as she walked through Market Street towards the castle.

Market Street was the epicentre of Lumiere and Amelia's favourite part of the city. Lumiere looked like a fairy tale, or a dream. It was a dream, of sorts: Amelia's great-great-times-something grandparents designed the city themselves after the previous one was ravaged by one of those wars disguised as a marriage. Wait, no, this one was a war disguised as a war.

Neither grandparent was particularly conventional when it came to architecture, so every corner of Lumiere demanded your attention. White stone buildings rose into spires with forty sides, each one mosaiced with tiny chips of glass or ceramics. Colourful tiles trimmed every window and door, forming intricate patterns that drew the eye in a hundred directions. Only a few windows in each building held clear glass: almost everywhere boasted a stained-glass frieze of pictures or spirals. Even regular stone walls were round and misshapen, like someone plucked all the cobbles from the street and piled them on top of one another until they resembled a building. On every wall in the kingdom, from the tiniest cupboard to the largest battlement, hung a looking glass. No one was sure who had started the tradition, but they all appreciated how easy it was to check if you had food stuck in your teeth. Brightly painted doors, each competing for attention in violent shades of fuchsia or lavender or buttercup, were elegantly latticed with wrought iron. Some buildings were mosaiced entirely in silver, others in turquoise or tangerine. There wasn't a grey space in the country and according to rumour, every colour in existence had been pressed into use somewhere in the kingdom. A staple of every primary school education in the Kingdom of Mirrors was a day spent naming the colours of each public building.

On some walls Amelia passed, mosaics formed cheery squares like kitchen tiles. On others they made bright, childlike images telling the history of the Kingdom of Mirrors. There were the olive trees, there was a woman brewing a potion, there was a boat next to some fish. The mosaiced fish were consistently bigger than the little people on the boat, which always made Amelia wonder whether the artist had no sense of scale or if they wanted to emphasise how brave the fishermen were, sailing out to face enormous krakens and territorial mermaids and climate change.

As she walked, Amelia gazed across Market Street to the little boats in the harbour, bobbing about on a minuscule breeze. Something moved near the hull of a dinghy, perhaps a school of fish or a merperson. The boat's owner dozed on deck, oblivious. Up in the hills, lights twinkled from the peaks of each mountain. Lime green parakeets hollered over tiny sparrows, shouting over hulking seagulls.

Amelia stopped at one of Market Street's twenty food carts to buy a snack before lessons. After a small diplomatic incident in which a local butcher replaced fresh lamb with fresh cat without mentioning it to anyone first, Amelia had lost her taste for kebabs, so she chose a cheese pastry and orange juice, praying that the cheese came from a farmyard animal. 'You don't have to pay, Your Majesty,' the vendor told her as she rummaged through her purse. Although Amelia was dressed exactly like her subjects in a loose cotton dress, and had the same umber skin and jet-black hair, the market knew her well. She frequently hid there to avoid going to the castle.

'Of course I do…' Amelia searched for the vendor's name. 'Sarah. Of course I have to pay, Sarah, I'm not going to go around stealing from my own people!' *Especially when you're one of the few tradespeople who pays their taxes,* she added silently.

'Well, if you're sure… can I put some magic in it, on the house?'

'Oh, go on then.' Amelia yawned and fanned herself with her sunhat. 'Something to revive my desire to go to my maths tutorial.'

Sarah smiled and reached under her little counter for a vial labelled *enthusiasm: medium strength.* She flicked a couple of drops into Amelia's orange juice. 'Bad day at the office, Your Majesty?'

Amelia gazed across the square at children her own age. Walking home from school with cloth satchels slung over their shoulders, wearing faded patterned dresses or shorts, they jostled each other along in a way that always struck Amelia as very comradely. She tried to push back a pang of jealousy. Until Amelia's father suffered a stroke when she was twelve, Amelia attended the same local school, wearing the same faded patterned dresses. Amelia hadn't especially enjoyed formal education when she was forced to go, but after years of squeezing in private tutoring between royal business and gradually losing touch with her friends, Amelia would have given anything to spend eight hours with other people her own age. Especially since public schools let children take a class in brewing potions, and Amelia's parents wouldn't let her near any magical substances since an unfortunate encounter with a dog and a growth potion when Amelia was ten.

'Oh you know…' Amelia shrugged. 'Eighty per cent of our teachers and healthcare professionals have gone abroad in the last five years and we can't afford to train anyone new. There's also a shortage of sorcerers who know how to bewitch the weather, so we're in for a long summer.' She scowled and chomped her pastry. 'Oh, and the Earl of Star's Reach spent half an hour telling me how he plans to convert an entire room in his house into a shrine to the gods of gratitude. Gratitude! He'd do better praying to the gods of lost causes.'

Shrines in the Kingdom of Mirrors were like pairs of shoes: everyone owned at least one, but to people who considered themselves fashionable, they were the ultimate status symbol. Each building housed a shrine to one god or another, made from chips of mirrored glass or colourful tiles. Some were the size of a post box, others the size of a shed. Some people, like the Earl of Star's Reach, dedicated an entire room in their house to their shrine, replacing all the windows with stained glass and filling the room with candles, incense and tiny prayer scrolls. The Earl fancied himself a priest and a magician… the rest of the court fancied him a nuisance, especially when his attempts at magic resulted in a castle-wide evacuation.

'Is he thinking of going for any particular design?' Sarah asked. Her kiosk's little shrine to the water gods was the size of a milk jug and made from blue glass chips. It sat on the till, which Sarah had bewitched to open only when she touched it.

'The Earl wants a plain mirrored mosaic floor in the shape of his family crest to remind him of his respect for the gods of hearth and home,' Amelia recalled. 'But his wife doesn't like to be reminded of her mother-in-law.'

'Maybe she should pray to the gods for a new husband, then,' Sarah suggested. 'Or send him south to Scavenger's Ruin. The Sapphire Dragon will take care of him.'

Amelia tried to laugh, but something stuck in her throat.

She finished her food at the communal iron tables, soaking up the atmosphere as the evening sun reflected off the mirrors on each building, casting the entire street in strange beams of light and duplicating the market one thousand times over. When she was little, Amelia thought that every mirror contained another world, where another Amelia sat, looking into another mirror.

The temperature was starting to drop, so Lumiere was coming alive. Children scampered around fountains while parents chatted at cafés. Amelia could hear restaurants getting ready for the dinner shift, lighting fires to roast lambs and goats on spits, and she could smell oregano and bougainvillea plants. A cicada chirruped somewhere, almost drowned out by a marching band performing at one end of Market Street. The band appeared to be in direct competition with an orchestra holding a performance at the other end of the street. Babies' cries mingled with dogs' barks as street vendors contended with everyone. 'Salted olives, a jar for a silver coin!' Amelia could get two jars of olives for a copper coin; there were more olive trees in the Kingdom of Mirrors than there were people. A wasp buzzed near Amelia's pastry wrappings, close enough to count its legs. She waved it away. Another vendor hollered, 'Feather pillowcases, collected from swans this morning!' Very few swans lived in the Kingdom of Mirrors. Possibly the manufacturer had plucked several pigeons.

It was well past time to go to lessons, so Amelia hauled herself from her seat and brushed her sticky hands on her dress as the loudest voice of all cut through the crowd. 'Magical gold amulets—guaranteed to keep your marriage healthy! Just five gold pieces for two!'

Amelia stopped at the stall, waving another wasp away from her face. Anything for another two minutes of fresh air. 'What do those amulets do?'

'They spice up your marriage, Your Majesty.' The vendor, a sun-wrinkled old man called Harry, bowed when he recognised her.

'*My* marriage?'

'Or your parents' marriage!' Harry seemed to remember who he was talking to. 'Not that the King and Queen need any help in their marriage! I am sure they're blissfully happy!'

'Yes, blissful,' Amelia agreed. She rubbed her temples. The enthusiasm was taking its time kicking in. 'Couldn't the marching band and the orchestra perform at different times?'

'Course they could,' Harry grunted. 'But that would be too easy. The orchestra is starring in a musical.'

'Remind me never to see it,' Amelia muttered.

'You might want to, Your Majesty, it's about the war with the Sapphire Dragon.'

'Why on earth would I want to watch a musical about the war?' Amelia demanded. Why couldn't people stop bringing it up? First Sarah with her joke, now Harry. For ten whole minutes as she strolled through Market Street, Amelia had forgotten all about the war her people waged against their unfriendly neighbourhood dragon.

Harry shrugged. 'Search me, Your Majesty, I've never been much of a theatre person. Can I interest you in a shell for calming headaches?'

'No, no, I'll take a tonic later on.' Amelia knew that Harry's 'magic shells' came from Lumiere's beach. Although blood red and very pleasant as a table decoration, they held absolutely no magical properties. Amelia didn't have the heart to tell him she knew the scam: not everyone in the kingdom was a magic user. Amelia never quite got over the fact that her mother, Queen Hazel, excelled at casting protection spells, while Amelia, Nicholas and their father, King Emmanuel, possessed about as much magical ability as a pair of socks.

She left Harry there as he called into the market once more. 'Magical shells! Endorsed by the Princess Amelia!'

Miraculously, Amelia arrived earlier than her tutor. Madame Louisa taught every subject on a different day in their little room at the very top of the castle tower. Ten floors up, Amelia could still hear the orchestra and the marching band battling it out. While she waited, she flicked through the pile of newspapers they'd used for her current affairs lesson the previous week. There was the war, *again*, on almost every page.

'*The Sapphire Dragon razes another town!*' screamed one headline. '*Is he heading north from his cave at Scavenger's Ruin?*'

'*King Richard of the Valley of Dreams sends more troops to the Kingdom of Mirrors' aid,*' announced another paper. '*Meanwhile, King Emmanuel has borrowed money from Queen Margaret of Stormhaven to pay for another siege at Scavenger's Ruin, to force the Sapphire Dragon from his stronghold.*'

'*King Richard's troops are killed in a failed siege of the Sapphire Dragon's lair,*' bemoaned the most recent. '*The latest failed attempt to oust the Sapphire Dragon, who has laid waste to the south coast of the Kingdom of Mirrors for 20 years, brought the military death toll up to 32,892 troops, and the civilian death toll to—*' Amelia stopped reading. She knew the numbers already.

What really depressed her was that these newspapers could have been from any year in the past two decades, ever since the Sapphire Dragon blew in from the Western Ocean on a terrible storm. Villagers spotted him curled on the beach at Scavenger's Ruin, a fishing town at the southernmost tip of the kingdom. According to survivors, his wicked blue scales reflected the sun and his wicked grey claws left welts in the sand. Fire spat from his nostrils as he torched every building in sight, along with most villagers. War was declared immediately, of course. There's a saying in the Three Kingdoms: *sticks and stones might break your bones but they don't do squat to dragons, so you'd better bring something stronger.*

Everyone was hopeful for the first few years. Hundreds of well-trained soldiers marched south each spring, although barely fifty would make it back, and most of those spent months in the Lumiere hospital being treated for horrendous burns. The navy lasted precisely fourteen minutes, which was how long it took the Sapphire Dragon to incinerate the entire fleet. The Valley of Dreams, the Kingdom of Mirrors' closest neighbour, sent troops and extra weapons. Dragons are creatures of habit and prefer to live in secluded, enclosed spaces, so the Sapphire Dragon existed mostly in the hard-to-reach caves below Scavenger's Ruin, venturing out occasionally to hunt fish from the once-plentiful sea or to meet the latest contingent of soldiers. Once or twice a year he would fly north, razing more towns and extending his territory just a little bit closer to Lumiere. Within some six years of the dragon's arrival, half the nation was inhospitable and hundreds of terrified families had fled to Lumiere. Others went further north still, to the Valley of Dreams.

Lumiere soon started to creak under the extra pressure from its new inhabitants. Tensions built up in crowded communities as the war dragged on. After a few more years of state funerals for fallen soldiers and emergency aid relief for refugees, someone cracked and threw a brick into the tent of a refugee family, starting the famous Midsummer Riots. Amelia remembered watching the carnage from her bedroom window as a terrified six-year-old, counting the fires that spread across the city. 'Dad will sort it out,' twelve-year-old Nicholas assured her. 'He has an army.'

'He doesn't,' Amelia argued. 'They've all been eaten by the dragon.'

'The Sapphire Dragon doesn't eat people,' Nicholas assured her. 'He just sets them on fire.'

Amelia refused to go near a lit candle for weeks after he said that. Emmanuel and Hazel finally bowed to political pressure and began to borrow money from Queen Margaret of Stormhaven to train even more soldiers. They signed an agreement with the Valley of Dreams, allowing thousands of refugees to relocate to safer lands in exchange for access to the Kingdom of Mirrors' ancient magical scrolls, something no monarch had allowed for centuries. Eight years later, the kingdom's debts were crippling its economy and all those extra soldiers proved about as effective as a comedian at a funeral.

'Your Majesty!' Amelia jolted out of her reverie as Madame Louisa swept into the room. 'Apologies for my tardiness. Let's get started with some mathematics!'

Madame Louisa didn't set particularly difficult exercises today —but then, Amelia recently balanced Louisa's family's bank account. Amelia scratched away at algebraic fractions, trying not to think about dragons. She glanced out the tower window. All the way up here she could see the entire city, nestled amongst the mountains and olive groves, temple spires sparkling. People would soon be making their way to evening prayers, if not just stopping for ten minutes to light a candle in the nearest shrine. If she had magical vision, which wasn't unheard of in the Three Kingdoms, she could see around the coast, all the way down to Scavenger's

Ruin. From this distance the road looked like it was scratched into the mountain by a dragon's claw. Her fist clenched around her pencil. Would she ever go anywhere without being reminded that her kingdom was on its knees?

The pencil snapped. Across the room, Madame Louisa raised her eyebrows and handed Amelia another.

Chapter Two

'Lovely fish soup, Dad,' Amelia ventured, as she sat down to dinner with her parents later that evening. The family ate in the ancient, draughty castle kitchen. Ever since the head chef and kitchen staff moved away to find jobs in more prosperous parts of the Three Kingdoms, her father assumed the role of castle cook. Amelia could see zero olives, which meant he was having a good day. After his stroke, Amelia took on most of his responsibilities so Queen Hazel didn't need to double her workload, but he insisted on running the kitchen. Across the table, her mother attacked a loaf of bread and tried not to raise her eyebrows. Amelia dipped her spoon into the bowl. 'Wow. I can really smell… garlic?' King Emmanuel was an enthusiastic chef, but the people of the Kingdom of Mirrors generally survived on what they could afford, which was bread and olives. There are a great variety of ways to serve bread and olives, but they all require imagination, which King Emmanuel ran out of around the same time his teenage daughter took over his job.

'Garlic is the only thing that makes the fish seem fresh,' her father said sadly. 'I mean, er, it is fresh. Of course. It came from the harbour… yesterday.' Amelia knew it had come from the harbour a week ago because she was the one who went out with the kingdom's little fleet of fishing boats to see what was left in the sea after so many years of the Sapphire Dragon helping himself to its fish. She also knew how much effort it took for her father to be able to stand at the kitchen counter at all, so she tucked in.

As they ate, the family went through the day's business. 'As you know, Emmanuel, Queen Margaret sent messengers last week to remind us we owe another portion of loan repayment,' Queen Hazel said, 'but Amelia managed to persuade her to give us until the winter solstice.' Amelia was surprised at Queen Margaret's leniency. King Emmanuel had put off asking Stormhaven for money until after the Midsummer Riots because no one did business with Margaret de Winter unless they wanted to spend the rest of their lives feeling like a fly trapped in a spider's web. Stormhaven was the northernmost and richest of the Three Kingdoms, and its ancient matriarch ruled with a personality far colder than her name.

Queen Margaret travelled all the way south when Amelia was small; Amelia's abiding memory of the visit was the elderly monarch's icy stare and enormous fur coat, which she insisted on wearing even as the midday sun melted windows and one of her servants fainted from heatstroke. Amelia never saw Margaret emit a bead of sweat. Rumour had it that she slept with a dagger under her pillow, had locked one of her nephews in a dragon-guarded tower and planned to rule from beyond the grave via an Ouija board and a set of tarot cards, despite a kingdom-wide ban on magic use. Amelia believed every rumour.

'How much does Margaret want for this instalment, exactly?' King Emmanuel asked. He had his daughter's wide brown eyes and awkward shoulders. When they smiled, they were copies of one another: all teeth and lots of dimples. Neither had smiled recently, and although Emmanuel was only fifty, he could have passed for Amelia's grandfather.

'She has demanded five hundred gold bars,' Amelia replied. 'Unfortunately, we have zero gold bars. Do you think she would take the equivalent weight in olives?' she asked. She was only half joking. The Kingdom of Mirrors' olives were famous throughout the Three Kingdoms and the nation's most popular export. Just last year Amelia traded a quarter of the state's olive oil stock for a thousand cattle from the Valley of Dreams.

'The only language Margaret speaks is money,' her mother sighed. She sipped some soup, winced, then looked at the table. 'Of course, Amelia, Queen Margaret would be very happy to marry you to one of her sons or grandsons.'

'No.' Amelia said flatly.

'Amelia…' her father began.

'No.' Amelia uncovered an olive and stabbed it. 'How many times do I have to say no? You can't just marry me off to clear our debt!'

Her parents did not mention that they could. Nor did they mention that her older brother had been happy to marry himself off until fate threw him off course. They didn't need to.

'Oh, we've had another message from the merpeople,' her mother added. 'The dragon has taken two more children this summer. Parents are starting to move north to safer waters.'

'That's all we need,' Amelia groaned. 'Half the population of merpeople in the harbour won't make life difficult for anyone. '

'They've suffered as much as we have,' Hazel pointed out. 'And they can't just move to dry land.'

'Thanks for mentioning that, it hadn't occurred to me!'

Hazel raised her eyebrows, which suggested Amelia had better stop arguing, so she spent the rest of the meal in silence and excused herself as soon as the plates were washed. She wandered the castle for half an hour and found herself back in the classroom at the top of the tower, staring at the newspapers. The Kingdom of Mirrors was once a prosperous, vibrant nation known for its lively street festivals, beautiful architecture and delectable sea food. Her parents weren't to blame for its terrible fortunes. But if no one did anything about the dragon, the war and their debts soon, there would be no kingdom left to rule when her father died. Which, a tiny and horrible voice in the back of her head whispered, would probably be sooner rather than later.

Irritatingly, Amelia wouldn't be in this position at all if not for her annoying brother.

Because she grew up with an older sibling, Amelia was never expected to shoulder a large portion of royal responsibility. Throughout her childhood she was taught the basic requirements of being a good princess—how to make small talk with someone who has bad breath, the best way to throw a dinner party for politicians with special dietary needs, the fastest way to stab an adversary with a longsword—then left to her own devices. But when Amelia was twelve, Prince Nicholas embarked on the customary coming-of-age quest that all wealthy, promising young men undertook when they reached their mid-teens or decided they did not enjoy academic study.

His quest was to ride north to the castle of Queen Margaret of Stormhaven and choose one of her many offspring to marry (or her offspring's offspring—there were enough of them to choose from). In return, Margaret would cancel half of the Kingdom of Mirrors' debt. He was to rid one of Stormhaven's many mountains of a pesky goat-eating lion on his way, just to prove his worth. Instead, Prince Nicholas killed the lion on the slopes of Traveller's End Mountain and, when a local goat farmer named Raphael made Nicholas dinner to say thank you, he decided to marry him. Although marriages between royalty and commoners were perfectly normal in the Kingdom of Mirrors, Nicholas wanted to live on the mountain with his husband and their goats rather than inherit a large, hot kingdom filled with olive trees and refugees, so he abdicated. Most of the kingdom protested: marrying below one's station is one thing but rejecting public duty to become a farmer (albeit with the title Duke of Lumiere) is quite another. Gossip columnists complained that Princess Amelia was even less tameable than her brother, although critics agreed that at least she would have decades to practice being queenly.

King Emmanuel had his stroke six months later.

Amelia and her mother did a pretty good job of running things with the help of their High Council, but they spent most days wondering how much longer the kingdom could go on without defaulting on their loans. A few years ago, Amelia hadn't even known what the phrase 'defaulting on loans' meant, and she hadn't cared. Why couldn't her brother have quested to the south coast instead of heading north? He could have killed the dragon like a good prince was supposed to do and *then* gone on some little journey to rid Traveller's End Mountain of that lion. It wasn't even a magical lion, Amelia thought bitterly. It was a standard, boring mountain lion. She was even more annoyed with herself for missing having him around the castle. He would have liked Harry the amulet salesman, and he always made royal engagements feel like an adventure instead of like a piece of complicated homework.

Amelia tidied the newspapers and organised a few textbooks, just for something to do. Her favourite history book, *The Magic, Mayhem and Mystery of the Kingdom of Mirrors* was dog-eared and out of date, but the author had recently moved north and was now focusing on researching the Valley of Dreams' historical association with the wine industry. Then there was *The Monarchies of the Three Kingdoms (and how two of the kingdoms managed democracy)*, and *Sorry, Dragons Don't Really Die, But Here's How You Can Try*. Amelia scowled at it. Down on Market Street, a trombonist started a solo. A second later, a cellist started one too. Why on earth were they *still* playing music? It was night-time! When Amelia became queen, her first Royal Decree would be a change in live music laws. She pulled *Dragons Don't Die* from the shelf, angrily sweeping past the sections on Ruby Dragons, Emerald Dragons and the Lesser Spotted White Gold Dragon. There was the section on the Sapphire Dragon:

Sapphire Dragons are not the largest of the dragon family, nor the most dangerous. They can't spit poison and their eyes won't paralyse you. They do not eat people. Unfortunately, what they lack in strength they make up for in cunning: it is hard to outwit a Sapphire Dragon, and their only known weaknesses are their sensitive ears and delicate eardrums. They cannot stand high pitched sounds at great length, and if anyone were to shoot an arrow into the ear of a Sapphire Dragon, they would surely slay it, as the opening of the ear is the only part of the Sapphire Dragon's anatomy that isn't protected by a layer of scales. No one in human history has ever come close enough to try, though.

Their sensitive ears.

An idea hit Amelia like a beam of sunlight.

Before she could think too much, Amelia hurled herself down the tower stairs and through the castle, so quickly that the stained-glass windows started to blur together. Her parents were sitting in the smallest drawing room with cups of wine. The king worked through his physiotherapy exercises while the queen read a book about strategic negotiations.

'I have a plan to slay the Sapphire Dragon!' Amelia gasped as she skidded to a halt on the rug, narrowly avoiding the wine cups.

Her parents looked up. 'Amelia,' her mother chided, 'can't this wait until tomorrow? Your father can't take too much excitement.'

'I hardly think a conversation with my daughter is bad for my health,' the king murmured, although he didn't look entirely convinced. 'Does this have anything to do with your plan to build a giant water cannon and fire it at the dragon?'

'I made that plan *ages* ago,' Amelia said dismissively. 'We don't have enough equipment to build a canon powerful enough. This is a new plan.'

'All right,' Queen Hazel shrugged. She had the same long afro hair as Amelia, but while Amelia braided or tied up hers to keep it away from her face, Hazel wore a new style or accessory every week, refusing to fire her hairdresser even as they cut down every other expense. She also remade all her dresses, so she looked like she had a new outfit for every occasion, but it was really the same material, redesigned four or five times a year. Even curled in a frayed armchair, she looked more like a queen than Amelia ever would. 'Let's hear it.'

Amelia took a deep breath. 'Well, the reason the kingdom has had to borrow so much money over the last twenty years is that we're fighting a war we can't win, *and* the entire population of the south of the kingdom moved north *and* the bottom dropped out of the tourism industry. That's correct, isn't it?'

'Correct,' her father agreed.

'*And* the reason for the war, refugee crisis and tourism trouble is that the Sapphire Dragon razed every village on the south coast and is sitting at Scavenger's Ruin right now, setting fire to anyone who tries to kill him. That's right, right?'

'Right,' her mother sighed.

'And it's entirely possible that, were the dragon to disappear then the war would be over and within three to five years, and assuming we ran a sustainable tourism programme and ploughed proceeds into rebuilding towns, life as we once knew it would return.'

Both parents nodded.

'In that case,' Amelia said. 'It's time the dragon disappeared.'

'Oh, well, I'm glad you've thought of that,' Queen Hazel said with a wave of her hand. 'We've spent twenty years thinking that we quite like having him around.'

'Mother!' Amelia was stung. 'I'm only trying to help.'

'We know that, Amelia…' the king said gently. 'But if we knew how to kill the Sapphire Dragon, we would have done so by now. Dragons can't be killed easily. Or at all. Do you really think we haven't tried everything we can think of?'

'Of course not!' Amelia said quickly. 'It's just, you're going about it all wrong.'

Queen Hazel's eyebrows did a complicated dance. 'How, exactly, are we going about it all wrong?'

Amelia steadied herself. *Please don't let them laugh at this please don't let them laugh—*

'Wasps at the food carts in Market Street don't sting all the people to make them abandon their food. They just buzz around until people are so irritated that they go indoors to get away.'

'Um, yes,' Queen Hazel said. 'But I don't think we can get rid of the Sapphire Dragon with wasps.'

'We need something more annoying than wasps,' Amelia pressed.

'Mosquitoes?' her mother suggested.

'Fish soup?' her father asked.

Amelia rolled her eyes. '*People.* People are so annoying! They yell at you about feather pillows, they insist on selling you fake amulets and they play their trombone at the same time someone else is trying to play the cello! What's the *most annoying* thing you've ever heard?'

'Oh, that's easy,' her father replied. 'It was the time you and Nicholas decided to form a jazz band. Half the castle got tinnitus.'

'I think the most annoying thing for me was when our seamstress had quadruplets,' the queen mused. 'None of them would sleep at the same time, remember? For months, you could always hear a baby crying. Eventually you thought you could hear a baby crying even if it was quiet. I thought I would go insane.'

'Some would say you did,' the king said amicably. The queen stuck her tongue out at him.

'So what you're proposing is that we can just *annoy* the Sapphire Dragon into just getting up and flying somewhere else?' King Emmanuel asked.

'We can if we make everything he hears ruin his delicate ears.' Amelia held up *Dragons Don't Die*. 'The Sapphire Dragon's ear canal and eardrum is the only unprotected part of its anatomy.'

Her parents looked at each other. It was the same look they exchanged when Nicholas brought Raphael the goatherd home.

'How do you propose we make enough noise to ruin his hearing?' King Emmanuel asked.

'We hold a festival.'

'A festival?' the king asked. 'For... for whom? The dragon?'

'For our long-suffering troops down on the south coast! This year is the twentieth anniversary of the dragon's arrival. Our brave soldiers deserve a traditional Kingdom of Mirrors festival honouring their work and sacrifice. So I'm suggesting a three-month event—'

'Three *months*?' Queen Hazel asked. Her eyebrows did another dance.

'Three months,' Amelia continued, 'of sporting events for the soldiers, each one with its own marching band. Three months of accompanying orchestral performances, street theatre, opera shows, circus events. Three months of *jazz music*.'

She knew she was onto something, because her parents exchanged another look. It was the one they exchanged at Nicholas and Raphael's wedding.

'All right,' her mother sighed. 'Call the Council to meeting.'

Amelia smiled as she swept from the room to find parchment to write notes to the High Council, calling them to a breakfast meeting the next day.

When Amelia was queen, she would commission a new mosaic for the castle's walls, depicting how she defeated the Sapphire Dragon.

Chapter Three

The next morning, the High Council assembled around a huge olive wood table in the Great Hall, tucking into jugs of iced coffee, stacks of fresh croissants and plates of fruit. King Emmanuel's specialty was breakfast; unlike most teenagers, Amelia had great enthusiasm for getting out of bed.

After Amelia's great-great-times-something grandparents won their war, the Crown rescinded absolute power to a publicly elected High Council of eleven people plus the monarchs—or ten people, if there was only one reigning monarch. An uneven total of councillors ensured there was always a tiebreaker… and someone to referee impromptu football matches. The citizens of the Kingdom of Mirrors lived, peacefully, for generations… until the Sapphire Dragon arrived and the fairy tale ended. At present the High Council had four non-royal members, only three of whom held Amelia's respect. The other seven members travelled south to slay the dragon the previous year and were now incapable of leaving either their hospital bed or their coffin. The kingdom hadn't held elections to replace them yet, because they were running out of suitable candidates; some muttered that Prince Nicholas should be bullied into returning to royal life. Still, Amelia called them to the richly decorated hall because she felt the occasion warranted pomp and circumstance. Queen Hazel took her seat next to Amelia and selected a croissant. King Emmanuel sat in a spare chair, watching his daughter carefully.

Most of the morning's pomp and circumstance was supplied by Lord Donald Fitzpatrick, who earned his title by saving a young Prince Nicholas from drowning in the harbour on a day out. In the seventeen years since then, Lord Donald had done little else to distinguish himself except wear spectacularly expensive clothes, which he purchased from the Valley of Dreams with sales of a book written about the twenty seconds he spent hauling three-year-old Nicholas out of two metres of water. Amelia would never understand how he had been elected four times without ever venturing to the south coast to help slay the dragon.

'Thank you for coming,' Amelia began when they were all assembled. Next to Lord Donald sat Baroness Theodora Rosewater, a business-woman elected to the council after years of running the most successful fishery in the kingdom, employing six hundred people. These days she oversaw the entire kingdom's fleet of fishing boats. Next to her, sipping glasses of orange juice, sat twin sisters, Ladies Elisa and Beth Montague. They had inherited an ailing olive grove forty years previously and within a decade they trebled olive oil production, invented a new type of olive press and married, then buried, a total of four husbands between them. Amelia could never remember if Elisa had three husbands and Beth one, or the other way around. Amelia took a deep breath. 'We have a new plan to slay the dragon.'

She outlined her idea, and when she was finished her parents nodded encouragingly. The twins looked faintly impressed and Baroness Theodora was tapping the hilt of her butter knife against the table thoughtfully. Only Lord Donald appeared uninterested.

'Your Majesty, apologies for not understanding...' he did not sound particularly sorry. 'But surely it is too dangerous to take simple musicians into the war zone?'

'Well, my lord, we've tried slaying the dragon the traditional way.' Amelia deliberately slowed her speech. 'Or some of us have, anyway. Clearly it has not worked. So we are embarking on a new strategy, em-ploying the wonderful skills of regular townsfolk. Who will of course be trained in self-defence. And heavily guarded. As we can't bully the Sap-phire Dragon into leaving our lands, we will persuade him to go using more peaceful means.'

'I don't understand.'

'I know you don't.' Amelia's mother coughed into her serviette. 'I know you don't understand *yet*,' Amelia corrected, 'but you will. You might want to take notes, my lord, because I have quite a detailed plan...'

Explaining plans, it turned out, was quite boring. Over the next few weeks, Amelia went through her idea with every council member at least twice, then got the kingdom security services involved. Eventually, af-ter weak points were highlighted and second opinions asked for, backup plans formed and every potential situation analysed with surgical pre-cision, the Council voted anonymously on Amelia's plan. Amelia was highly put out when she remembered that someone needed to abstain to ensure a majority rule; she was more put out when she realised that the fairest option was to abstain from voting on her own plan. Honestly, democracy. Her plan passed; four votes to one. Amelia smiled tightly at Lord Donald and asked him to have signs drawn up:

'TWENTIETH ANNIVERSARY WAR RELIEF GAMES AND FESTIVAL STAFF WANTED.

Are you a chef, baker or greengrocer? Are you a skilled plumber, carpenter, blacksmith, surveyor or architect? Visit the Royal Castle immediately. YOUR SKILLS CAN HELP OUR TROOPS! Volunteers must be able to reach the south coast in good health and be willing to stay there for a minimum of two months before the war relief festival begins, then a further three months for the duration of the festival. Volunteers are welcome to bring their families and loved ones to enjoy the festivities and will be given an allowance of gold to do so.

P.S. No one will have to live within two miles of the Sapphire Dragon. There will be armed guards. We promise.'

Uptake was slow at first, but gradually a queue began to form outside the castle. Amelia could hear Harry flogging crystals to visitors: a few chefs, some construction workers, a couple of olive farmers. Amelia saw Sarah the pastry vendor with her daughters, signing up eagerly. Some families had fled twenty years ago and were more than willing to return home; others just wanted to get out of the city before the summer heat set in.

After a week or two, once Amelia was sure people were willing to consider returning to the south, she designed another sign:

'TWENTIETH ANNIVERSARY WAR RELIEF GAMES AND FESTIVAL: ENTERTAINERS NEEDED.

Have you got a set of skills or hobbies that could entertain our troops? Visit the Royal Castle immediately. We are especially interested in: musicians, circus performers, opera singers and actors. Volunteers must be able to reach the south coast in good health and be willing to stay there for a minimum of three months. Volunteers are welcome to bring their families and loved ones to enjoy the festivities and will be given an allowance of gold to do so.

P.S. No one will have to live within two miles of the Sapphire Dragon. No, really. There will be armed guards. We absolutely promise.'

Harry flogged more amulets while the marching band and the orchestra signed up, shooting one another filthy looks as they queued. Within two weeks, Amelia counted about five hundred entertainers, plus their families.

Finally, Amelia designed another sign and sent it to the army camp at Scavenger's Ruin:

'INTRODUCING THE TWENTIETH ANNIVERSARY WAR RELIEF GAMES AND FESTIVAL!

In this 20th anniversary year, by order of the High Council, Scavenger's Ruin is holding a festival and sporting games to honour you, our brave troops, and your efforts to slay the Sapphire Dragon. All service people will be given four months' leave, effective immediately, to train for and participate in sporting events, and to enjoy the festivities.'

Word came back almost immediately. The soldiers were delighted to have some time off, and could the castle please send a list of participating sports? Would duelling be allowed? Amelia smiled and wrote back that yes, duelling was absolutely allowed.

'Come on you lot!' Amelia called from her horse a week later. 'We only have three more weeks until your group leaves for the south! I heard a dud note there!'

In front of her a ninety-piece orchestra, many of its members from that first orchestra in Market Street, sweated underneath a canvas shelter. Their conductor sipped iced water and asked nervously, 'Your Majesty, I must ask again. *Why* are you holding a festival?'

'We're doing something nice for our troops!' Amelia explained for the thousandth time, to the thousandth bewildered entertainer. 'It's about time we had some life in the south of the kingdom, and life means music! The Kingdom of Mirrors used to be famous for our festivals, and we deserve to be famous for them again.' The ninety-piece orchestra looked like it disagreed. *'There is a dragon on the south coast,'* she heard one flautist whisper to another. She tried not to imagine outlawing the flute.

'After you've gone through your music, I want you to practise Emergency Plan F Sharp,' Amelia reminded the conductor. 'We might need it if things go wrong.' The conductor nodded and wiped sweat from the bridge of her nose.

'They're not going to like it, Your Majesty,' she murmured with a glance at the flautist.

'Well, I don't like ninety-piece orchestras, but here we are!' Amelia beamed, gritted her teeth and trotted off to the next group of volunteers: a fifty-strong group of surveyors, architects and builders, enlisted to create temporary concert venues and housing for the entertainers.

'Ladies and gentlemen!' Amelia began, tossing her braids over her shoulder.

'Actually, Your Majesty, we're all gentlemen,' murmured a blacksmith near the front.

'Really?' Amelia asked, 'how awful. No wonder there are so few women in the construction industry. When this is over, I want an apprenticeship programme set up in schools to encourage participation in science, technology, engineering and maths. Anyway,' she continued, 'I have an important job for you all. In one week's time, you will move to the tip of the south coast to discern which buildings can be used for the festival, and design new concert halls, arenas and accommodation. Your new buildings will be temporary as we plan to rebuild the original structures eventually, but for the purposes of the festival we need Scavenger's Ruin to look like a proper town again!'

'Your Majesty,' asked the smith who'd spoken earlier. 'No disrespect, but why are we relocating *so* close to the Sapphire Dragon? Couldn't we just move the troops further out of the town for the festival so it's safer for everyone?'

'Good question.' Amelia had discussed the exact location of the festival with the Council at length and decided that the workers, of all people, deserved an explanation for the insane levels of danger she was asking them to walk into. 'Look. Scavenger's Ruin is where the dragon first arrived all those years ago. It's where our troops are based. They live there all year round. It's only right that we're based there too, to show our respect—and so we can offer proper relief and entertainment. Everything will be at least two miles away from the Sapphire Dragon's cave. We've trebled the number of magic charms on Scavenger's Ruin, and we've doubled the number of security workers. I can't tell you that it's completely safe.' She looked the blacksmith in the eye. 'But I can tell you it's as safe as we can possibly make it.'

'It's a suicide mission,' someone muttered. Amelia took a deep breath. It was tempting to explain that the real reason the festival needed to be so close to the dragon was to annoy him into flying away, but the less the general public knew of her plan, the less they would complain if it went wrong. If this didn't work, there would be serious calls to bring Prince Nicholas back from Traveller's End Mountain and reinstate him as crown prince, goat farming predilections or not. There was no way she would give her title back to her irritating, duty-abandoning brother. She would never live it down at family parties for one thing, and for another she wanted to get him back for that time he told her girls were terrible at running the country. He was about thirteen at the time, but still.

Her plan had to work.

Chapter Four

Amelia insisted on accompanying every consignment of workers and entertainers on their three-day journey to the south coast, so she came to know the route rather well. Head out of the city on the main road, take a left at Beth and Elisa Montague's olive grove. Follow the coast until you spot Scavenger's Ruin, a village nestled above a spectacular and ancient set of caves and beaches on the southern tip of the kingdom. Keep going until you reach the military tents.

Everywhere they passed on that first ride south, Amelia saw evidence of communities the Sapphire Dragon had driven away. Fishing boats lay abandoned on the side of the road next to crumbling nets and single oars. Every mile or so a cluster of little houses, all with bright stained-glass windows and winking mosaic roofs, sat near the beach. Every one was empty. Some gardens held sagging washing lines or crumbling shrines. Others had old horse carts or animal pens that were too big to carry north. Sometimes, Amelia saw bones.

By the time they reached Scavenger's Ruin, there was not a single person on the road. Amelia had a sudden and chilling thought that this was what the Kingdom of Mirrors had looked like before humans arrived, and this was what it would look like when they all died out.

The first workers to arrive were received with healthy suspicion by the army. Amelia insisted on meeting every regiment personally and tried to remain upbeat even when she heard someone whisper, 'I can't believe we're being ordered to go to parties by a teenage girl.'

'I can't believe you're being rude about your future head of state,' Amelia replied loudly. 'Would you like to follow my orders or would you like me to send you to meet the dragon in his cave?'

No one made any comments within her hearing after that.

Amelia's workers spent the first week surveying every charred building and spare piece of land. Most stone buildings had survived surprisingly well, but everything smelt like ash. Some soldiers carried little bottles of scented oil around to mask the odour, or cast protection charms around their faces.

It was soon decided that an old inn, the Magnificent Hotel in the centre of town, would act as Amelia's headquarters; it was one of the few buildings that seemed to have survived the dragon's wrath with its stairs intact. Miraculously, Queen Hazel managed to track down the entrepreneur who used to run it. He was now settled in the Valley of Dreams, running a sweetshop and expecting his third great-grandchild, and he informed the castle by carrier pigeon that he was perfectly happy to let the Kingdom take what remained of his hotel. 'Just make sure you remove all the lizards,' his letter concluded. 'It was hard enough to get them out when we cleaned regularly.' Amelia didn't mind lizards—the Sapphire Dragon was the only scaly creature she had a problem with—but for her idea to work, what remained of Scavenger's Ruin had to look impeccable, so they spent the second week deep cleaning everywhere they could reach, scrubbing dirt from mosaics and evicting lizards and rats alike.

By the end of the third week, Amelia had a plan of where everything was going to go. By the end of the fourth week, tents were installed in the largest public square and Amelia allowed herself an evening off, sipping cocoa on the porch of the hotel while construction workers' families wandered the streets, pointing out old landmarks. A squeaking sound interrupted her moment's calm.

'Your Majesty?' it was Major Guerrero, Amelia's Head of Operations. Or Vice Head of Operations, since technically she was in charge. The Major could have retired years ago (and probably should have). Over the twenty years he had been shooting poisoned arrows at the dragon and threatening him with swords and cannons, Major Guerrero had relinquished one foot, six fingers and half a lung to the Sapphire Dragon, and now travelled using a wheelchair and specially fitted oxygen tank. He carried more weapons than anyone Amelia had ever met and inspired equal amounts of fear and amusement from his troops, so Amelia couldn't think of anyone better for the job of organising a festival.

'Major,' Amelia smiled. 'How goes the orchestra tent work? Did the pegs sit in the ground properly? I know the earth isn't ideal.'

'The boys say it'll hold, Your Majesty, although they recommend we only use it for gentle activities. No exuberant dancing. They've had a look at the old school and think it could be a good place to set up the awards ceremony for the troops. The soldiers are taking the sporting events very seriously, ma'am.'

'I would expect nothing less from our fine military. Where can we host the circus performances?'

The Major tapped a knife against his palm. The remains of his hands were blotchy with burn scars. 'They will have to be held in a bigger tent, slightly further out from the main town. There's an old quarry that might work.'

'Excellent. Oh, and Major, I don't want you to forget about the fire precautions. A fire cart on every street corner and dragon safety training for all our workers and entertainers. No exceptions. Make sure the protection spells covering the entire town are tested against something of the dragon's size and weight. I know they won't hold for long, but they should give us time to evacuate if things go wrong. Are we clear?'

The Major twinkled. 'Yes, Your Majesty. By the way, your mother told me to pass on a message about Stormhaven.'

'Is Queen Margaret coming to visit?' Amelia asked, alarmed.

'No, no... apparently a Stormhaven family arrived in Lumiere yesterday morning, seeking asylum.'

'Someone wanted to seek refuge... *inside* the Kingdom of Mirrors? Why on earth would they do that? We can hardly feed ourselves.'

'Well, quite. According to your mother's message, the family are claiming that they had to leave Stormhaven because they are magic users.'

'Magic is banned in the north,' Amelia said slowly. 'But I've never heard of anyone fleeing because of it. I wasn't aware Margaret was especially tough on offenders.'

The Major shrugged. 'Maybe she's cracking down? Or maybe this family just got tired of living up in the mountains.'

'Maybe. I'll write to my parents today. I'm going back to Lumiere in a week or so for some classes with my tutor... thank you for telling me, Major, I appreciate it.'

'Of course, Your Majesty. You know, I'm rather glad your brother went off with that shepherd. I like the way you do things.'

'Raphael is a goat farmer,' Amelia corrected, but she tried not to smile.

At the end of the fifth week, the games began.

The Opening Ceremony was fairly small, given that there were no spectators other than the troops and the families of the people who worked at the festival, but Amelia insisted on holding an event, with a jazz band, to declare the festival open.

'People of the Kingdom of Mirrors,' Amelia announced from a small platform. She had worked with one of the engineers to create a tiny wooden mouthpiece that would amplify her voice for the crowd. She rather wished she had commissioned a magical dress that didn't make her sweat in the evening warmth. Was her voice always this squeaky or was it the amplifier? She was going to blame the amplifier. She swallowed. 'Welcome to the Twentieth Anniversary War Relief Games and Festival. We are here to honour our troops, those who are with us and those who—who—aren't, and we're here to remember that we used to know how to have a good time.' Amelia coughed. 'So, er, have fun! I do declare this festival open!'

'Not bad,' Queen Hazel murmured as the crowd headed to the opening act: a performance from Amelia's favourite orchestra. Amelia felt warm in her toes. Queen Hazel's compliments were like rain after a drought: rare but refreshing. 'I think the amplifier needed a bit of work, though.'

'Oh,' Amelia smiled. 'I'm working on that.'

At dawn the next day, the sport began.

Amelia didn't consider herself particularly athletic, although she was fairly fit from going up and down the castle stairs all the time and enjoyed rowing out on the open sea. She took self-defence lessons once a week, which usually felt less like exercise and more like preparation for the inevitable. Her brother was better at conventional sports; as a teenager he ran sprint relays in the Three Kingdoms' five yearly sporting games. These soldiers were something else entirely: bored with the monotony of camp life and under constant stress from the possibility of another dragon attack, they spent most of their time training or playing sport against each other. The result was several hundred highly dangerous soldiers, all nursing carefully honed competitive streaks.

Each week featured different assortment of sports: polo, sprinting, long distance running, javelin, discus, archery. Then bare-knuckle boxing, assault course events, and, of course, duelling. Some events were specifically for the magically gifted: a flying carpet race, a levitation competition and a contest to see who could brew the smelliest potion in thirty minutes. Amelia lost count of activities. She was slightly irritated that there were no aquatic events, because no one could work out how to build a swimming pool without compromising Scavenger's Ruin's ancient plumbing system, but she promised herself that if her plan worked and the villagers returned, she would build them a proper leisure centre.

The troops loved the entertainment that came with the games. Every soldier was given an allowance to spend on whatever they liked—most tried food carts and restaurants, or the newly renovated steam baths, which Amelia commissioned after seeing the army's excuse for a shower block. The troops' allowances were the last of the treasury's gold and Amelia tried not to wince as she counted it out. Very few soldiers had seen an opera or a musical, so at first the performance tents were full mainly of curious faces. Street theatre, on the other hand, was a national pastime. Every outdoors play sold out. A hum settled over Scavenger's Ruin as chatter and music and productive people sounds started to overtake the cicadas.

One afternoon, when Amelia was walking home from a ballroom dancing event, she stopped to examine one of the fire carts she had stationed at every street corner. Its huge tank was full of seawater; Amelia could hear it sloshing gently as the cart rocked in the breeze. The firefighter on duty, a stout woman who sat on the top of the cart reading from a spell book, levitated a cup of tea that glowed bright purple. She smiled in recognition at Amelia, who tried not to think about how fun it would be to learn to do magic properly, at a university in the Valley of Dreams or with one of the witches who lived out by the olive groves in the east of the kingdom. The closest she came to magic day-to-day was when she prayed at her portable shrine. It was the size of a goblet, held a single stubby candle and had burn marks up the side. Some of the mosaics had chipped off, so the Durante family crest, a gold set of stars over a fish on a cyan background, looked like a frog with a headache.

'Did you see that play the other day with the man who ate knives?' one soldier asked his friend as they passed. Amelia shrank into the shadow of the fire cart, too hot and sweaty to be sociable. She recognised the soldier from the archery tournament: he placed first, winning a dukedom. His new land consisted of about four olive trees and a hut, but no one on the High Council could think of anything except land to give away as prizes.

'Brilliant,' his friend agreed. Amelia realised with a lurch that half of her face had the patchy, stretched skin of a third-degree burn. One of her eyes was covered with fabric. 'You know, I thought this festival was a bit insensitive, bringing all these people down to the dragon, but I'm glad Princess Amelia started it. My parents used to tell me how good our festivals were, and I never believed them.'

They strode off. The firefighter beamed down at Amelia from her post.

At the end of the ninth week, troops spotted the Sapphire Dragon perched on the furthermost rock at Scavenger's Ruin, watching them like an oversized eagle. Amelia ignored the shivers down her spine and extended the festival by another month, adding more sporting events and introducing a dog show and comedy nights. Each event was carefully staggered, so there was rarely a moment between sunrise and midnight when you couldn't hear a song, a monologue or a crowd cheering.

Amelia forced herself to remember that life would continue after the festival, so she began to split her time between Scavenger's Ruin and Lumiere, catching up with lessons and castle business while Major Guerrero kept watch on operations.

'You know,' her father said one evening as they played chess, 'I think this plan might have more than one benefit. Have you noticed how much happier people are now they know we're holding festivals again? Your mother told me that old Harry the amulet vendor has started filing his taxes.'

'Miracles do happen,' Amelia said dryly. 'Actually, we have noticed that regular citizens have been coming down to the south coast. And they're spending money while they're there... I think people just want something to talk about that isn't the war. Hey, no cheating!'

Her father shrugged innocently. 'Cheat my own daughter to victory? Never. By the way, we've had more refugees from Stormhaven.'

'More?'

'Eight families in total. Three with small children. One elderly couple who are now in the infirmary recovering from exposure. I think we might have to call a meeting with the Valley of Dreams. They must have noticed something similar—they share a border with Stormhaven after all.'

Anxiety squirmed down Amelia's neck. 'Let's send word to Nicholas and Raphael. They might know something.'

Her father nodded. 'Don't let this distract you from the dragon.'

'I won't, but...' Amelia felt as though she were back in science class puzzling over an evasive problem. They were missing something about the refugees, or about Stormhaven, or both. She scowled at the board and her father smiled sympathetically.

'A monarch's work is never done?'

'Yep. Hey, I said no cheating—'

Her father cackled horrendously. 'Checkmate!'

Back at Scavenger's Ruin, tourists arrived in ever-increasing numbers. Soon hundreds of people came for a day at a time, making the long journey down to the coast and back again, until the High Council voted to open several inns, inviting entrepreneurs to set up tour companies and better transport links. Soon townspeople outnumbered soldiers, lounging outside cafés or wandering the streets, reapplying enchanted sun cream and queuing for souvenirs.

'People are visiting at an increasing rate of roughly thirty per cent per week,' Baroness Theodora reported at the weekly council meeting. 'We've opened six inns, and so far ten different restaurants have opened just outside the camp. The produce suppliers have had to advertise for more staff. We've also had a request to allow magical earplugs to be sold in every inn,' Theodora added. 'Your Majesty, people are finding it hard to sleep with all the extra events and night life. Some people are convinced that they actually can't manage to find silence anywhere in the festival.'

'Ah, they're just paranoid,' Amelia shrugged, although she allowed herself a moment of self-congratulation. 'We want people to need earplugs to leave the house. Grant the permission, and make sure I get a pair. What I'm more interested in is infrastructure. Can we power all this extra industry? Is it safe with the dragon so near?'

'The Major has made a list of buildings we can use,' Elisa put in, 'and we're looking into felling old wooden timber huts from the north of the kingdom to use as material for new buildings. The wood had been earmarked for rebuilding the navy, but I think that can wait.'

'Recruit more fire stewards,' Amelia said. 'I don't want a single square foot of the town without protection. And find more guards. Just—just in case. Oh, and Theodora, I want to make sure Emergency Plan F Sharp is ready to go, wherever we are.'

'Yes, Your Majesty. Should we—' Theodora hesitated. Over the other side of the table sat Lord Donald, the only council member Amelia hadn't trusted with her most precious of backup plans. He was busy polishing his pocket watch. 'Should we make sure there is a, a *device* with every musician?'

Amelia nodded. 'At all times, Lady Theodora. We can't be too careful.'

The Princess and the Dragon

Chapter Five

Once they had verified all the extra safety features of the festival, Amelia felt confident enough to write letters to dignitaries in the Valley of Dreams and Stormhaven, inviting them to watch the games and sample the entertainment. Queen Margaret's entire family and most of her court declined, of course, but King Richard of the Valley of Dreams came to stay at the Magnificent Hotel for a few days with Queen Florence and their children, Prince Richard Junior and Princess Beatrice.

Richard Jr. was the only other royal Amelia's age, but he looked younger and always gave the impression he had been surprised to learn he was heir to the throne of a medium-sized kingdom. Possibly he was spiritually weighed down by his mother, who said very little and only ever wore black. Amelia was painfully aware that she should know who Queen Florence was mourning, especially since she was Queen Hazel's third cousin and the two were very close, but she always got her royal stories confused and there is no polite way to ask these things.

Richard was a laugh, though, once you got him to relax a bit. 'What's the Sapphire Dragon like?' he asked after dinner, the evening before his family left for the Valley. Richard had some school exams to do, but the family had promised they would come back to sample the rest of the attractions. Amelia thought Hazel and Florence just wanted an excuse to go out for drinks. Amelia and Richard stood outside the Magnificent Hotel, waiting for a carriage to take them to the opera, which neither of them were particularly excited about. Unfortunately, Amelia had promised to attend every event she staged.

Amelia considered before answering. The Valley of Dreams was almost as magical as the Kingdom of Mirrors, but dragons did not live there... unless you counted the old magicians who taught in the universities. She gazed across the street at a kiosk selling emotion-flavoured ice cream.

'I don't actually know,' she admitted. 'I've only ever seen him from a distance.'

'Probably scarier than musical theatre,' Richard mused, adjusting his large, wire-framed spectacles, 'but less scary than Queen Margaret.' He looked at the sky for a minute, like he was deciding whether to say something. Amelia waited. 'You know, it's really cool what you're doing here. In the Valley of Dreams everyone who wants to inherit their parent's title has to go on a coming-of-age quest to prove they're worthy of becoming a lord or a duchess or whoever, but most people just go and fight a baby hydra in the mountains or trek up into a forest to find some long-lost gold. No one does anything this brave.'

'Um. Thanks.' Amelia wasn't sure what she had expected Richard to say, but that wasn't it. 'Um. I'm just doing what's needed. I mean, I also want to prove I'm worthy of succeeding my father. Don't tell anyone I said that.'

'Well, you get my vote for queen any day.'

They watched passers-by for another minute.

'Hey, Richard,' Amelia said suddenly. 'In the Valley of Dreams, you all use magic, right?'

Richard nodded. 'It's not quite like here. Magicians teach people who are born with magical abilities in our universities, but you have to be really good to study under them. Most people just know a few charms or spells for every day, to help with chores or in the vineyards.' He looked at Amelia with curiosity. 'Why?'

Amelia swallowed. How much could she confide in Richard? They were basically cousins, but Amelia knew that he had never had to assume his father's duties. He probably spent his days playing polo. Well, maybe not polo. Maybe something you could do sitting down, like backgammon. 'We've heard rumours about Stormhaven. Apparently, Queen Margaret is cracking down on magic users. Have you heard anything unusual?'

Richard shrugged ruefully. 'They don't confide in me. The court, I mean. I'm not very good at all that.' He wore the same worried look as his mother. 'I'll keep my eyes open,' he said suddenly. 'You'll be the first to know if I do hear anything.'

'Cheers,' Amelia smiled. 'I mean, thank you, Your Highness, I am much obliged.' Richard burst out laughing.

The opera was quite rousing, although neither Amelia nor Richard understood much. They hung around afterwards meeting the cast and passed on their parents' best wishes. 'They would have loved to have come,' Amelia explained, 'but they've taken Princess Beatrice to an open-air pantomime.'

The conductor sniffed. 'A pantomime? Well, I must say it's gratifying to see young people enjoy operatic music. May I offer you my card? We perform at anniversaries, birthdays… weddings.'

Amelia and Richard looked at each other.

'Lovely,' Amelia managed to say. 'I'll be in touch if I ever know someone getting married.'

She avoided Richard's eye until they were back in the carriage.

After the royal visit, to Amelia's great surprise, tourists from the Valley of Dreams came to the Kingdom of Mirrors to visit the festival. Some took a tour, staying in Lumiere for a day or two before travelling to the south coast. Others stayed in one place for a week or two before moving on, soaking up the summer sun and exploring the Kingdom of Mirrors' architecture and famous seafood dishes. Artists started illustrating tourists' meals while they ate and selling them the pictures afterwards as a souvenir. One of Theodora's fishermen caught an octopus, and tourists stood at the harbour to bid for the chance to have it cooked by a Lumiere chef. Amelia would never understand northerners, but she gave the fisherman the night off.

Four months in, as the sun fried everything it touched and the festival wore on, the treasury took enough gold to make an early loan repayment to Queen Margaret. 'One payment of five hundred gold bars down,' Amelia said grimly to Lady Elisa as they saw off the carriage containing the riches. 'Only about eight hundred payments to go.'

Elisa clicked her tongue and reapplied spell-protection-factor sun cream to her nose. 'You just put more gold in that carriage than we've paid Margaret for three years. I think there's a lot to be hopeful about.'

Amelia smiled, but she was wary of getting too excited. The Sapphire Dragon could still swoop down on the festival and incinerate them all.

Speaking of dragons: their enemy still had not moved from his nest in the caves at Scavenger's Ruin except to hunt, but Amelia went to sleep every night expecting to be woken by the sound of wings swishing overhead. There was no way to avoid the music and noise of Scavenger's Ruin now—she could hear it hours before she arrived, all the way down the road from Lumiere. But what if she misjudged? What if they just irritated the dragon until he got up the energy to invade and break through all their safety spells?

Coincidences are the spice of life, probably, so the next day the Sapphire Dragon sent a message.

Chapter Six

As a rule, dragons do not communicate with their human neighbours. What is there to communicate when the tenant can eat the landlord? But unwelcome news greeted Amelia in her room at the top of the Magnificent Hotel at dawn, when she was woken by Baroness Theodora.

'Pardon me, Your Majesty, but we've heard from him.'

'Heard from whom?' Amelia yawned. Why was she always wearing her rattiest pyjamas when she had visitors?

'The Sapphire Dragon, Your Majesty. He wants to parley. With you.'

It was ridiculous, really, that Amelia hadn't expected this sooner. The Sapphire Dragon, like all good magical creatures, could carry out basic conversations. He just hadn't chosen to in the past twenty years, and Amelia hadn't considered that he might change his habits. 'All right,' she said. 'I'll get dressed and go to see him.'

The opening to the dragon's cave was only reachable by sea, so Amelia hauled the remains of the kingdom's navy, a small wooden dinghy, to a hastily constructed jetty. The charred remains of five or six other jetties stuck out from the sand. Major Guerrero insisted on coming along for the ride, even though it took ten minutes to get him, his oxygen tank and a miniature shrine into the boat, before Amelia rowed them from the beach to the cave opening. The limestone rock and sunlight transformed the water from normal blue into an iridescent cerulean, so it looked less like seawater and more like a spilt potion. In some places the water was darker, like sapphire. Amelia shivered.

They took a white flag of truce with them and, officially, no weapons. The dragon might, maybe, possibly, *just* want to talk and get spooked by a large display of firepower, so Amelia just had one enchanted knife hidden in her sleeve and another in her breeches, plus a small flare in her pocket, just in case. The Major would be staying in the boat, but he held a wicked bow and wore a quiver full of poisoned arrows and more flares. If things went really wrong, Amelia reflected as they neared the caves, they could always cause an explosion with the Major's oxygen tank.

The Sapphire Dragon's home was a giant rabbit warren hidden beneath rocks, the only human-sized entrance looking out onto the ocean and partially submerged at high tide. As the boat neared the opening, Amelia took a deep breath. This was it. She checked her knives were in place, then threw an anchor onto a bit of protruding rock. She hoped it would hold— she didn't fancy swimming home.

'Good luck, Your Majesty,' Major Guerrero said quietly. Amelia could only nod. Her voice seemed to have abandoned her completely. The Major trained his bow onto the cave mouth. 'If you need any help, just set off the flare.' Amelia nodded and pulled herself off the boat and onto the rock. Striking a match against a wooden torch, she took a tentative step into the narrow opening. It was more of a tunnel than a traditional cave. It was dark, too dark to see without torchlight, but there was a glimmer of light at the other end. She forced herself to keep moving, wondering vaguely how terrified she would be if she *hadn't* taken a bravery potion with her orange juice, and took another step, then another, and before she could breathe—

She was in the dragon's cave.

Amelia knew from her research that this cave was several thousand years old, and that the stalactites, formed by limestone and salt, grew at a rate of one centimetre per year. She knew that at least one species of bat lived here, alongside dozens of flocks of pigeons. She knew that the water inside the cave system (a mixture of freshwater and saltwater) would, in a couple of weeks, trickle through a cave on the other side of Scavenger's Ruin. None of that knowledge prepared her for the cave's beauty.

Although the Sapphire Dragon had the ocean for his front garden, he had a private pool to himself. This cave was inaccessible to people but by the tunnel Amelia had come through; his entrance was a gaping hole in the cave roof, left by a long-ago earthquake. Local legend said that the earthquake was caused by a water nymph, so angry with her cheating husband that she literally screamed the roof down. Like the sea outside, the impossibly-still water glowed luminescent blue in the sun. If she hadn't seen it with her own eyes, Amelia would have believed it synthetic, lovingly created by a magician whose brief was to create *blue, but glowing*. The sky above looked grey in comparison. If not for the stench of dead fish or her sense of impending doom, Amelia would have loved it.

Oh, and if not for the fact that curled on an outcrop in the centre of the pool was the Sapphire Dragon.

Amelia's first thought was that he was just a really large, really colourful lizard. Then she took another step forward and realised he was so much more. He was bigger than the Magnificent Hotel, with a thick scaly body and long tree trunk tail. His feet were like a crocodile's, except each foot was the size of a dustbin lid. Each claw was larger and sharper than the knives Amelia carried. He tasted the air with a forked tongue that was longer than Amelia was tall, and she could see multiple rows of teeth, each one shaped like a knitting needle. His wings were tucked behind his back, but Amelia guessed his wingspan must have been twice the size of him, at least. He shifted, ever so slightly, and a chink of light caught his scales. Amelia caught her breath. Each scale was larger than the gemstones in Amelia's mother's crown, and each was a slightly different shade of blue: some rich navy, others bright cobalt. He made the blue of the water look like a child's colouring game. Some scales were shiny like actual gemstones, while others were dull and clouded. No arrow or sword point in the world, no matter how magical, would penetrate that armour.

The Sapphire Dragon opened his eyes.

They were yellow—luminous like some of the fish off the coast of Kingdom of Mirrors—with an oily black pupil that reached from eyelid to eyelid.

'Princess…' the dragon hissed, and the hairs on Amelia's neck stood up. His voice was like nails dragged across a cheese grater. 'Why are you at Scavenger's Ruin?'

Amelia stepped forward and heard something crunch under her boot. She risked a glance downwards. Little bones littered the cave floor. Some looked suspiciously like baby merpeople.

'Why are *you* at Scavenger's Ruin?' Amelia asked. She hoped she sounded brave. She hoped she had cleaned her teeth properly. The dragon hadn't.

'Two decades ago I sent every single human on the south coast packing,' the dragon hissed. 'This is *my* home now. Why have you chosen to return?'

Amelia shrugged. 'This land still belongs to us. Our soldiers have been stationed here for twenty years. They try very hard to kill you, if you don't mind me saying, and I wanted to do something nice for them.'

'They work hard to kill me,' the dragon mused. Amelia thought she could hear him laughing, but that might have been waves lapping the sides of the cave. 'They do not succeed.'

'True,' Amelia acknowledged. 'But we want to do something nice anyway.' An idea came to her, so she risked inching forward another step. 'You know, if the relief festival goes well, we might even move some industries down here to take advantage of all the empty space and military knowledge. Artificial intelligence, maybe, or tech support.'

'Tech support?'

'You know, if you have a problem with the well at the bottom of your garden then you send a carrier pigeon to the tech support centre down here and they send you a message back explaining how to fix your well.'

'Wouldn't it be easier to just speak to a local well engineer?' the dragon hissed. 'Surely a support team can't actually tell what's wrong from hundreds of miles away. What if the messages take ages to send and receive? What if the well needs fixing by a specialist?'

'We haven't settled on the details yet,' Amelia admitted. 'But we're also considering trying to revive the tourism industry. *Lots* of people have enjoyed coming south to visit the festival so far.'

'The tourism industry? But… I'm here.' He shifted on his haunches and Amelia nearly went for her knives. *No violence*, she reminded herself.

'Well, yes, but people like a bit of sun and sea on their holiday. Especially the Stormhaven lot who spend all their time up in the mountains. Besides, there are other draws except you. We have the stunning sunsets, the peace and quiet away from everyday life… it's perfect for families! We're thinking of setting up a resort and a few schools. There's even talk of a performing arts college…'

'Performing arts college?' Amelia thought she saw the dragon pale. 'Please tell me you aren't doing musicals as part of this festival.'

'Of course we are! We started with that one about a revolution. You know, the one where everyone dies. It's a bit dreary for me but audiences seem to like it. There's another one opening next week actually—'

'I have heard enough, girl! Leave my cave at once before I fry you.'

'It was nice to meet you,' Amelia said as she backed away, turning only at the last second to clamber through the tunnel and back into the boat.

The dragon exhaled fire over the space where she'd stood.

'You know,' Major Guerrero said as they rowed back to the beach. 'I think he liked you.'

'Hm.' Amelia thought for a minute. Her heart was pounding and her hands shook a little as she rowed. 'I want to extend the circus's residency. And we need to get the blacksmiths to construct larger seating platforms. Let's bring more people in. And, Major—that device I had you install in every tent? I want them all checked. Each one needs to be working properly. I have a feeling our emergency plan will become our only option.'

'Very good, Your Majesty.'

When they got back to the beach, Amelia had a visitor. Standing on the jetty, looking like he needed a steam bath, was a familiar figure.

'Little sister!' Prince Nicholas beamed. 'You've grown. What a spectacular knife you're holding.'

'Nicholas! What are you doing here?' Amelia hugged her brother, who gingerly manoeuvred around her weapons.

'I got your invitation to the jazz festival, of course. I heard there's a running competition or two?'

'You've missed the running,' Amelia said with her head on his shoulder. He smelt very much like goat. 'There's still a couple of long jump heats. A few bicycle races. Some gymnastics. Where's Raphael?'

'He had to stay and look after the farm,' Nicholas said smoothly. 'He sends his regards. And, um, he made you this—' he reached behind him for a delicate leather bag and pressed it into Amelia's hands. 'It could carry all your knives.'

'Thanks!' Amelia took it eagerly. 'Have you seen Mum and Dad yet? Do you want to go to a street performance later?'

'Yes and yes,' Nicholas said as they walked along the pier. 'I stopped in Lumiere to say hello. They said they would be down in a couple of days for the jazz festival.'

The return of the Duke of Lumiere, only something that happened every summer and alternate winter solstice, was warmly welcomed by the king and queen but even more warmly by Amelia. Her brother was six years older than her, which sometimes felt like centuries when they were children. Now, with most of her days spent in the company of old war veterans and council members, Amelia realised how much she missed spending time with people born in the same decade as her.

'How's your food?' Nicholas asked Amelia one evening a few days later. The sun was setting over Scavenger's Ruin and the royal siblings were having dinner at a pop-up restaurant.

'Really good,' she replied, her mouth full of cheese. 'I sort of wish I could live off halloumi. Do you and Raphael sell your goats' cheese?' Amelia was always hungry for more information about her brother's life: he was a descriptive but inconsistent letter writer.

'Yep. Also hair and leather, like your excellent knife bag.'

'Do you like farming?'

'Do I like being awake at all hours on the slopes of a rocky mountain with fifty goats?' Nicholas sipped wine. 'Yeah, I love it.'

'And Raphael?

'I love him, too.' Only Amelia could have noticed the inflection in his voice.

'I meant, does he love it too? Is something wrong? With you two?'

Nicholas took another sip of wine. 'No. Yes. I'm thinking of coming home.'

'Why? Are you getting divorced? Do you want your title back?'

'No, and no. Well, yes—I mean, only if the people demand I return—'

'Oh, and they would, obviously,' Amelia snapped, voice rising. 'For gods' sake, I can *do this*!'

'Calm down!' Nicholas hissed. Fellow diners were starting to stare. 'This is not about you.'

He took a deep breath, and then another. Amelia speared a bit of cheese and chewed to give them both time to keep their tempers. Eventually Nicholas put his knife and fork down.

'You know magic is banned in Stormhaven.'

Amelia's curiosity beat her anger. 'What has that got to do with you?'

'Well, I still have a shrine and pray to the gods, which is technically illegal,' Nicholas explained. 'And, er, I can do this.'

He clicked his fingers and emerald light crackled from his fingertips, catching the candle on the table and turning its flame green. Amelia was immediately insanely jealous. 'How—when?'

'I think I've always been able to do conjuring, it's just that I've had time to practise up in the mountains.' Nicholas grinned. 'Now I can do loads of stuff.'

Amelia stared at the candle. 'What will happen if you're caught? I don't know much about Stormhaven law and order.' Amelia didn't know how much she should say about the refugees. You never knew who was listening in public—and she didn't want to worry her brother. She would call forward the meeting with the Valley of Dreams—could they speak to King Richard when he returned? She would have a book of Stormhaven law brought down to Scavenger's Ruin tomorrow.

'Magic isn't just banned in the north; it's taboo. If you do it, you don't talk about it.' Nicholas looked as serious as Amelia had ever seen him. 'Usually you get a prison sentence, but in the last few months there have been rumours… Rumours of people going missing, of prisoners who were never released. Children disappearing from the street—'

'*Children?*'

'Just rumours,' Nicholas said quickly.

'If you're thinking of coming home,' Amelia noted, 'you don't just think they're rumours.'

Nicholas said very little for the rest of the meal.

Chapter Seven

As the weeks wore on, tourists kept arriving in the Kingdom of Mirrors from further afield, spurred on by good reviews. One Stormhaven banker, who came to see Amelia cut the ribbon on a crèche for the entertainers' children, said enthusiastically, 'It was recommendation enough that our neighbours didn't get eaten by the dragon, but the entertainment facilities here are unbelievable! Have you thought about holding musicals?'

'We already have two,' Amelia replied, adjusting her sunhat, 'and two more are opening in a few weeks' time. Although, um, the Sapphire Dragon never actually eats people. He just sets them on fire.'

'Oh.' The banker shrugged. 'Well, I'll certainly be encouraging my friends to take a trip down here. Especially since it's easier to—' he swallowed.

'To what?' Amelia asked.

'Oh, nothing.' He was a smallish man with a receding hairline and a gut that suggested he drank Valley of Dreams wine more than he exercised. A small crease appeared on his ruddy forehead.

Amelia looked at him cannily. 'Were you by any chance going to say the words *it's easier to do magic in the south*?'

He blinked. 'Maybe.'

Amelia nodded. She had scheduled a summit with King Richard in the Valley of Dreams for the autumn and had set about collecting as much information about Stormhaven as she could in the meantime. 'I understand. Please do point your friends here if they would like... a break from normal life.'

He looked profoundly relieved. 'I will, Your Majesty, thank you. Now, could you point me in the way of the ticket office?'

In the end, it was the musicals that did it.

Five months after that first High Council meeting, it was the final night of Nicholas's stay. The whole family got dressed up to see the musical that inspired Amelia's plan in the first place. It was called *Claw!* and had already been open for several weeks; Amelia was only able to stomach it on opening night because she knew it had the potential to induce heavy auditory bleeding. The royal family of the Valley of Dreams was there too, returned as promised. Little Princess Beatrice clutched a stuffed toy replica of the Sapphire Dragon that was almost the same height she was. Amelia would never stop being surprised at the level to which toy makers would stoop to keep up with a trend.

This particular performance was more polished but more irritating: the first act ended with a family who lost everything to the dragon jigging their way into Lumiere.

Nicholas bought them ice cream in the interval, so when the lights went down Amelia was mostly concerned with not getting chocolate on the many ruffles of her pink evening gown. A bouncy number about refugees started up as shadows danced on the stage and walls. A musical was, Amelia decided as she dug the last of her ice cream from its undersized pot, quite a comforting evening out if you didn't mind hopeless optimism.

A dragon's shadow passed over the stage.

It wasn't part of the musical.

Amelia, up in the royal box, knew they had about five seconds before their protective spells broke, allowing the dragon closer. It was only due to the strength of the enchantments that he hadn't entered Scavenger's Ruin already. She leapt from her seat, grabbed her knives and flew down the stairs.

Somebody screamed.

With the grace of the kites Amelia and Nicholas used to fly above the castle, the Sapphire Dragon swept down to the stage, landing neatly on a papier-mâché statue of himself. Within a heartbeat he was methodically setting fire to every prop, every stage fixing and every empty seat. Each building in the camp had been enchanted to withstand fire and smoke damage, but human magic only works so well against dragon magic. In a few minutes, the air itself would catch alight. She heard Nicholas tell their parents and guests, 'Stay under cover,' then catapult after her. She hoped her father wouldn't try to move too quickly. The last thing she needed was for him to die of a heart attack as he tried to run to her aid.

By the time Amelia reached the stage, the cast had fled into the audience, and the audience was fleeing towards the exits. Fire stewards used a mixture of standard firefighting and magical firefighting, throwing water and sand on everything while muttering curses and flinging potions onto the flames. They were containing the danger—but were they? Someone was going to be killed in the stampede if they weren't all fried to a crisp.

Only the orchestra hadn't moved: sat in the pit between the stage and the audience, they couldn't leave without climbing the steps to backstage and walking directly into the dragon's path. They also had Amelia's strict instructions not to move in the event of a dragon invasion and they sat, mute, waiting for her command.

Please, she thought, *please let this work.*

'Emergency backup plan, Your Majesty?' asked the guard nearest to her. He held a sword in one hand and a bucket of sand in another. 'Which plan would you like us to implement?'

'Emergency Plan F Sharp!' Amelia gasped. 'Tell the entire festival!'

'On it, ma'am,' he said and bounded into the crowd, calling to his colleagues.

Amelia ran toward the dragon, who was turning his attention to the curtains above the stage. She moved one of her knives to the other hand and pulled her little amplifier from her dress.

'STOP!' Amelia yelled through the amplifier as loudly as she could. The audience froze and so, thankfully, did the dragon, who turned his yellow eyes toward her. Was it her imagination or did he look more tired than when they last met? His fires were swiftly burning through anything flammable, but the guards and stewards kept their heads and tossed sand onto everything. Out of the corner of one eye, Amelia noticed her father, safely down the stairs, herding people out of a side exit. Out of the other eye she saw her mother edge her way around the room, checking no one was hurt.

'Sapphire Dragon!' Amelia marched toward him, her knives quivering. 'Why have you laid waste to a perfectly nice theatre?'

'To end this,' he hissed, smoke spewing from his nostrils. The papier-mâché effigy collapsed. 'I cannot stand the infernal noise from you people any longer. I haven't slept in weeks. My head is pounding. I thought you were joking about the musicals.'

'I never joke about musicals.' Amelia wished she was wearing something other than her evening gown. It was her favourite shade of cotton candy pink, but there was no way she could fight properly wearing it. Thankfully she'd insisted on her trusty leather boots instead of the satin slippers her mother picked out. 'I warned you we wouldn't give up.'

'You did,' The Sapphire Dragon seemed almost thoughtful. 'I respect you for that. But now I must kill every person in this town.'

'Orchestras!' Amelia yelled into her amplifier. 'Jazz band! Anyone who's listening! Emergency Plan F Sharp! Go!'

Thank gods for emergency backup plans—and conductors. With a flick of her baton, the conductor unleashed Amelia's secret weapon, researched and practised in secret for months. On a count of three, every musician in the camp played the highest musical note physically achievable on their instruments. Individually, each sound made by each instrument was quite nice. Together, all Amelia could hear was pure noise—noise made higher and magnified by a little device Amelia had invented and installed across Scavenger's Ruin back at the beginning of the festival. As well as amplifying all sound, her invention created the highest note in the known world. Too high for people to hear, too high for dogs to hear. Perfectly easy for Sapphire Dragons to hear.

It is hard to describe exactly what the highest note in the known world sounds like, since we can't hear it. Perhaps it's an irritating wasp buzzing over your head for hours. Perhaps it's a couple shouting at each other in public all day. Perhaps it's your noisiest neighbour playing the most appalling music you've ever heard at three o'clock in the morning when you've got a migraine and an exam tomorrow.

Perhaps, Amelia thought as music rang out for five entire minutes, it's the most beautiful sound in the entire world.

During the first minute, Amelia held her breath.

During the second, Amelia realised she was about to pass out and inhaled deeply. She could taste burning wood. The remaining audience looked bemused. A couple of violinists paused to stretch their fingers, then resumed playing. Amelia's father continued sending people through the side door while fire stewards, soldiers and physicians ran through the other way. The dragon winced.

During the third minute, the dragon twitched, his eyelids fluttering as he swayed on the spot. A flautist collapsed from the effort. Amelia briefly felt bad for thinking uncharitable thoughts about the flute.

At four minutes, the dragon fell to his knees. The building rattled. Amelia gestured to the guards to put their weapons down.

At the end of the fifth minute, the dragon was writhing on the stage, foaming at the jaws.

Amelia strode closer, pressing her knife to the side of his head, quite forgetting it was useless. 'Do you surrender?' she demanded.

'I do!' the dragon gasped.

'If we stop playing this sound, you must leave the Kingdom of Mirrors forever, immediately. Do you understand?'

'Yes,' the dragon hissed. 'Just—just stop it!'

Amelia raised her hand and the orchestra stopped playing. She could hear every musician in the camp putting down their weapon. Someone rushed to the aid of the flautist.

The dragon staggered to his enormous feet. He was clearly incapable of focusing on anything and swayed heavily. After a couple of false starts, he spread his leathery, scaly wings and knelt into a crouch. 'Where will you go?' Amelia asked. She barely let herself believe they might have succeeded, but she also didn't like the idea of the dragon getting shot down over Queen Margaret's skies. He would end up in a zoo. Or mounted over her fireplace.

'Oh, across the sea, I think,' the dragon replied. 'Somewhere over the Eastern Ocean. There won't be any musicals there.'

Without another sound he beat his wings and rose into the air, gathering speed until he was a speck in the distance.

No one spoke for a moment.

'Well,' Amelia said, turning to the crowd. 'Let's get everyone to the hospital, immediately. Cancel every performance and make sure all our visitors get back to their lodgings. I want every guest book checked twice! We need to make sure no one is missing and no one was hurt. Use all magic carpets to transport the injured and get me a magician who can cast fire-containment spells. Dad—Father—Your Majesty! Please put that sword down. Could we get some more fire stewards and physicians in here please?' She could hear soldiers elsewhere in the camp, running through safety measures and checking who was hurt. 'Everyone please stay calm—' she broke off in a fit of coughing, her throat as dry as the Lumiere road. Possibly she had for once shouted a little too loudly.

'Everyone stay calm!' Nicholas continued, 'and follow the guards to the nearest exit immediately. Please allow priority to the injured, the young, the elderly and the orchestra. Do not return to your seats! Yes, sir, even you—could someone please get that gentleman's hat? He seems to have left it—Amelia! Get off that stage before it collapses!'

Amelia sprinted down the stage's wooden steps, wheezing, and joined the queue for the door, where she almost fell into—

'Oh, Your Majesty, please, you go first—' Sarah the pastry vendor stepped out of the queue and gestured for Amelia to go ahead.

'Hello Sarah,' Amelia said weakly. 'No, no, you were quite near the stage—is that ash on your dress? Where are your children?'

'Back at the pastry cart, Your Majesty, I was here on a night out.'

'Ooh! With whom?'

'Oh, just by myself. I haven't had the evening off for years.'

'Well, I hope you take more evenings in the future. Did you, er, enjoy the performance?'

'Loved it, Your Majesty, but I think you improved the ending.'

'Of course I did.' Now her heart wasn't about to explode with adrenaline, Amelia felt rather wobbly. Was this how the mosaiced fishermen felt after they defeated krakens and mermaids? Gods, it was overrated. Ten minutes of life-or-death action and she was ready to sleep for a week. After she had checked in with her parents and Major Guerrero, of course—and where was the Valley of Dreams royal family? She searched the crowd. There they were, with her parents and Nicholas, waiting for the crowds to file out before they left.

'Amelia!' Queen Hazel hurried over and enveloped her daughter in a hug. 'Are you all right? Never run with knives again!'

'Sorry. Yeah, I'm fine. Is everyone out?'

'Everyone,' the Queen confirmed. 'Let's get you to a physician—'

'Not until everyone's safe.'

'Okay, but then you go to bed, young lady. I don't care how many dragons you just slayed.'

'I suppose… technically I *defeated* him,' Amelia mumbled. Her head was starting to ache. 'Oh, forget it, I definitely slayed the dragon.'

Chapter Eight

Two days later, Amelia helped Nicholas lug his belongings to his horse. 'Come and visit us in the autumn,' he urged. 'You'd love the farm.'

'I want to.' Amelia replied, 'but I think I'm needed here. Dad's not getting any younger… and there are things I need to look into with the Valley of Dreams government.' She glanced down the road. At a respectful distance, loading their own belongings into a cart, stood Prince Richard and his family. They would see each other again in a couple of months for a summit about the Stormhaven refugees.

All around them, the military base was returning to normal. Festival workers were packing up, tourists were leaving. The carnival would be dismantled entirely over the next few weeks, and the military would follow soon after. They hoped to return permanent residents to Scavenger's Ruin by the winter solstice. It would be a long process, with a lot of travelling and hours of meetings with architects, but Amelia was ready for the challenge.

'Some of what you told me about magic in Stormhaven…' Amelia gathered her thoughts. She couldn't let her brother go back to Queen Margaret's kingdom without letting him know what might be in store when he got there. 'We've been hearing similar rumours from visitors. And, er, refugees.'

'Refugees? People have been fleeing *to* the Kingdom of Mirrors?' Nicholas exhaled. 'It must be worse than I realised. I've spent too long in the mountains…'

'How well do you know the Stormhaven Royal family?' Amelia asked.

'I abdicated my post and turned down one of her grandchildren to live with a farmer, and I do magic on a daily basis,' Nicholas replied. 'The only way I'll meet Queen Margaret again is if she arrests me.'

Amelia swallowed. 'Just keep your eyes open. Send word of anything… unusual.'

'Here, I got you this,' she added after a moment's silence. 'For your shrine.' She handed her brother a small, blue, glass dragon. Yellow citrine eyes winked up at them.

'I love it!' Nicholas hugged Amelia fiercely then pulled back and inspected her. 'You did an all right job, little sister.'

'Thanks,' Amelia swallowed. 'I think I'm learning how to be a queen after all.'

'You're going to be great. Never tell anyone I told you this, but... girls run countries better than boys do.' Amelia choked back a laugh.

Amelia's parents joined her as they waved goodbye.

'I just wanted to say, Amelia, well done for your plan.' Hazel's beady eyes smiled at Amelia. 'I was sceptical, but you've more than earned your place on the High Council.'

'Thanks,' Amelia repeated. She wasn't used to feeling like things might turn out all right.

'You'll be a powerful leader one day,' Emmanuel added. Before she could digest his compliment, he clapped his hands 'Right! Fish soup for dinner? Only joking, only joking...'

As well as a mosaic, Amelia decided as she turned away from the road, when she was queen she would commission miniature doll Amelias to destroy large toy Sapphire Dragons.

The Prince
in the Tower

Chapter One

In Prince Richard de la Fuente's experience, there were two types of hero: the storybook type, usually kind, intelligent and brave—if a little bit obsessed with marrying random princesses—and the type Richard had to entertain at his parents' garden parties. Richard enjoyed reading about the former—especially from a well-bound hardback while sitting in the bath—and despised the latter. Unfortunately, he almost exclusively mixed with the second group.

It was a sunny late summer afternoon in the Valley of Dreams, a couple of weeks after the family returned from the Kingdom of Mirrors. A gentle breeze encouraged relaxing activities like croquet and polite conversation about one's plans for one's house extension. The Valley, which Richard's family had ruled for generations, got its name from its delicious, potent wine. Carefully grown in vineyards and lovingly pressed by families with centuries of experience, the Valley's wine induced delightful evenings, pleasant dreams and nightmare hangovers. The kingdom's other great pride, its excellent universities, all offered packed courses on becoming the perfect sommelier.

By order of the King and Queen, the Valley of Dreams held nationwide garden parties twice a month during the summer. The entire kingdom ground to a halt for neighbours to sit with neighbours on picnic blankets, nibbling tiny sandwiches, sipping fragrant tea and admiring their hosts' gardening skills.

Usually on garden party weekend, if the royal family had their home to themselves, they would make pastries for their staff and sit in the shade of their ramshackle white stone palace on the edge of the Valley's capital, Laketown, playing board games and throwing tennis balls for the family dog, Bean, to chase. Unfortunately, today Queen Florence had organised a garden party for their fifty closest friends and dignitaries, so Bean was confined to the family's quarters lest he steal any food and Richard had to spend his afternoon on the lawn, pouring tea and listening to his peers boast about the heroic exploits they'd undertaken over the school holidays.

Take Lord Alistaire Eaton, for example. One successful quest to defeat a rogue chimera in the mountains and he thought he was God's gift to national service, despite being sixteen and having taken several armed guards who were rumoured to have done most of the monster fighting. And gods forbid you ever spelt his name as 'Alistair'... Then there was Grant Westborough, whose father, a count, recently bankrolled his trip to battle an army of sword-wielding republicans on the south border. Grant never passed a chance to remind Richard that *he* should have taken the quest, even though Grant knew full well that Richard had been semiconscious after a school sports accident at the time.

'Richard, may we have some more tea, please?' That was Grant now, beckoning to Richard with one finger. He had missed out his usual nickname for Richard, Prince Twitchy, as their parents were listening. Valley law required all children to attend state schools, so Richard was educated in socially diverse classes of thirty children, most of whom were uninterested in his title and a few of whom thought they deserved it.

'Of course,' Richard said quickly. In his haste to stand up he poured tea over the tablecloth. Grant raised one eyebrow, which reminded Richard that he wasn't fit to be Crown Prince and should probably hand the job to someone who was better at everything. Then he raised the other eyebrow, which suggested that someone was Grant.

Every encounter with someone deemed 'heroically dashing' by the *Valley Chronicle* made Richard more aware that if not for his parents, he would have been laughed out of court years ago for being a slightly chubby history enthusiast. Aside from his curly russet hair, which was the only part of his physique anybody had ever complimented and sounded like they meant it, Richard and the 'newspaper heroes,' as he privately dubbed them, had absolutely nothing in common. He could ride a horse and wield a sword, but not well. Definitely not at the same time. Richard was brave in his head, a valiant knight capable of slaying the worst of monsters, but in real life had no more chance of standing up to an enemy as he did of standing up to his mother when she made him wear crochet jumpers. By the time he was eleven, Richard had decided that any hero not found between the pages of a book was basically a villain with straight teeth.

'I can't believe it took a girl to take down the Sapphire Dragon,' Grant was saying to Alistaire over his tea. 'And Princess Amelia of all of them.'

Richard could believe it, as he was there at the time. In the weeks since Amelia's victory, the Three Kingdoms had barely discussed anything else. The majority of onlookers wanted to know how a hitherto uninteresting teenager came up with such a clever scheme; a minority pointed out that no one would have asked that question had her brother come up with the same idea. Mad genius, Richard reflected as he tidied up a cake stand and cleaned his glasses on his shirt, ran in Amelia's family. One of the castle groundskeepers was a cousin of Raphael the goat farmer. The groundskeeper still hadn't recovered from the fireworks Prince Nicholas and Raphael set off at their last New Year's Eve party. Apparently 'visible at thirty thousand metres' was an indication, not an outer limit.

'I rather thought one of the Valley of Dreams' court would have sorted out the dragon themselves given the strain all those refugees put on our resources,' replied Lord Alistaire, with a glance at Richard. *Oh, here we go,* Richard groaned inwardly. He was too inexperienced to go questing to another kingdom. Besides, the Sapphire Dragon had been the Kingdom of Mirrors' noisy neighbour, not the Valley's.

'Well, Alistaire,' simpered his mother, whose lilac dress gave her an unfortunate resemblance to the sugared cream cake she was eating, 'I'm sure the king had his reasons.' She glanced at Richard, who glanced at his father. King Richard merely shrugged.

'The Sapphire Dragon was not the Valley's problem.'

'It *was* the Valley's problem,' argued Lord Alistaire, 'when you consider the number of refugees we took from the Kingdom of Mirrors over the years.'

Richard almost choked on a biscuit. Arguing gently with the monarch while poking fun at the crown prince was one thing, but direct public defiance was quite another. The King was mild mannered, with a temperament that matched his sandy complexion and fondness for soft woollen slippers, but he was still the king. Richard waited for an outburst with bated breath. So, apparently, did Lady Eaton, whose cream cake lay forgotten on her plate.

'I'm sure King Richard had his reasons,' she breathed, her eyes on the king. 'Don't presume to understand His Majesty's logic, Alistaire.' Only Richard seemed to notice the slight inflection in her voice. *His Majesty has his reasons,* Lady Eaton was saying, *it's not our fault his brain is full of vine leaves.*

King Richard himself just inclined his head in Alistaire's direction. 'Perhaps you are right. But the new families have been splendid assets to the Valley of Dreams, and the dragon is gone now anyway...' he trailed off with a glance at his wife. Queen Florence was busy helping Beatrice remove a spider from the table, so Richard jumped in.

'Lady Eaton, how are your family's vineyards? It's been too long since we visited the north of the Valley. Am I right in thinking your land is on the border with Stormhaven?'

'Oh, Your Majesty, yes, our land backs on to Stormhaven—how good of you to remember. The vineyards are just fine,' Lady Eaton seemed relieved to be on safer ground. 'We've had a few issues with the villagers though, because of the Mad Prince. They insist he is stealing their belongings right out of their gardens.'

'The Mad Prince is just a rumour,' the king replied amicably. 'Queen Margaret would never lock one of her nephews in a tower. Especially not on Valley land. This prince is probably just someone's tidying-up spell gone haywire. They'll find all their possessions in someone's shed…'

'How do you explain the lights in the tower on the summit of Ghost Mountain?' Lady Eaton pressed. Richard got the impression that, unlike her son, she was looking for genuine reassurance.

'A lone shepherd, perhaps,' Richard offered. 'A priest who did a bad deal with the gods and went mad. Ghost Mountain has always been said to be haunted by bad spirits.'

Richard was too old to be drawn into conspiracy theories about haunted towers, but he was drawn in anyway. The rumours varied greatly: some people swore that an old magician with dubious mental health lived on Ghost Mountain and tried to commune with the gods on a regular basis. Others insisted an eccentric shepherd liked to wander around and scare underage locals who might use the mountain's craggy slopes to enjoy bootlegged wine. More people still stuck to the legend of the Mad Prince: that Queen Margaret had banished one of her nephews to the old tower as punishment for a horrendous crime. Some variations on the story suggested that the Mad Prince kept a pet dragon, or was guarded by a dragon, or was himself a dragon. The prince in the tower legend even had a cult following: a group of enthusiasts who called themselves 'towerians' and gathered every third Thursday to share theories and discuss the long line of eager young men who journeyed to the tower to prove their worth and did not return. It was their fault the mountain was called Ghost Mountain. Before rumours of the Mad Prince started, it was just called 'the big Eaton hill' after the family who lived nearby.

No matter what lived on the mountain, no one who ventured to the summit to confront it had ever come back to talk about their discoveries, so it was generally agreed that whatever lived there wasn't the sort of something you invited to a garden party.

'Alistaire, are you coming hunting later?' Grant asked Alistaire suddenly.

'Of course,' Alistaire replied without looking up, 'I have a score to settle with that family of wolves. I can't let them outrun me a second time!'

The rational part of Richard did not need to be asked on a hunting trip. He enjoyed neither hunting, violence, nor the company of anyone who would be going. The irrational part of Richard, which he tried very hard to bury under logic and reason, was desperate to be asked along too.

Lady Eaton was still discussing the Mad Prince with the king. 'I do wish someone would go up that mountain and sort him out! Our land is right at the foot of the mountain, you know, Your Majesty, it's very distressing for us.'

'I'll take care of it when I'm next at home,' Lord Alistaire said smoothly, as though he was away from his family's sprawling mansion on urgent political business, and not because he was a guest having tea at the White Palace.

'Thank you, darling,' Lady Eaton breathed.

'He's happy to be holed up in that old tower, whoever he is,' Count Westborough, Grant's father, said dismissively. His handlebar moustache nodded in agreement. 'Those types are insane, but quite content to be insane by themselves.'

'That's always what you think, until they turn up on your doorstep with a small army,' Lady Valentina Rathbone mused. Lady Rathbone was Queen Florence's sister, and one of Richard's few favourite aristocrats. 'Still, eventually one of these new heroes will train enough to quest to the tower and face whatever's in there! There's surely no rush if all this person's doing is spooking a few villagers. You young men all have plenty of time to prepare for a quest. Or young women, of course,' she said to Beatrice, who had safely evicted the spider and was chomping on baklava. 'Florence, I do love your roses. Do you use bone meal as a fertiliser?'

'Kitchen waste,' the queen replied. 'Lots of apple cores—'

'I'll go.' Richard heard himself say. One part of Richard's brain asked the other, *what are you doing?* The other part replied, *shut up and look like you planned to say that.*

King Richard looked as though he had sat on a bee. 'Pardon?' he asked, blinking rapidly. 'Richard, I think I misheard you—'

'I'll go up Ghost Mountain to the Mad Prince.' Richard repeated. 'I'll make it my coming-of-age quest. I have to do one before I'm sixteen anyway—'

'You're fourteen,' Lady Rathbone pointed out.

'Fifteen on the autumn equinox,' Richard reminded her. 'I'll go to Ghost Mountain and find the Mad Prince,' Richard insisted. 'I'll bring him back here so the court can decide if he's mad or bad or... something.'

The silence echoing along the table was a lot like the silence one hears when someone has admitted to stealing money from a charity box or leaving a baby in a burning building.

'Are... are you sure?' his mother asked, one fist clenched around the tablecloth. She looked paralytically worried, although she never really looked relaxed. Sometimes Richard's father would talk about how Florence had behaved before Richard's older sister Helena had died. He told stories of how she was very loud and very funny. Richard hadn't been born then, so he had to take his father's word for it. The Florence Richard grew up with was quiet, composed and always slightly uncomfortable around strangers. Now she studied her son as though looking for signs of terminal illness.

'Yes, I'm sure,' Richard said. 'I know I'm not the obvious choice, but Princess Amelia wasn't the obvious choice to slay the Sapphire Dragon either, and she did something better than that.'

'She conspired to move the Sapphire Dragon on to foreign lands, possibly ours,' the king pointed out.

'Yes, but she did it all without shedding a single drop of blood,' Richard argued. 'She used her initiative and it worked out better than anyone could have hoped.'

'And you think you're the best person to use their initiative?' asked Grant.

'Well yes, actually.' Richard said calmly. 'I haven't seen you use any initiative since you persuaded your father to pay for that trip you took to the southern border.'

Chapter Two

The next day Richard was beginning to wish he hadn't mentioned anything. His father, buoyed by the news that his son was finally taking an interest in physical activity, refused to allow Richard to undertake his quest until he took lessons with the castle's weapons master. 'Call them Prince-slaying lessons,' he said cheerfully from the doorway to Richard's bedroom at the crack of dawn, while Richard pulled his shirt on the wrong way around. 'You won't get a lie in when you're on your quest!' Bean padded in, ears askew. He yawned loudly then hopped onto Richard's bed, looking up at him sleepily as if to say, *I can't believe you voluntarily vacated this spot.*

'Neither can I,' Richard muttered, and headed down to the courtyard.

The lessons were as awful as they sounded.

No, they were worse.

His tutor was Madame Demetria, a diminutive Kingdom of Mirrors sergeant who had surrendered one eye and a foot to the Sapphire Dragon before retiring to the Valley to look after the nation's weapons collection. The first thing she did was ask Richard to list his skills. 'Essay writing,' he replied immediately, 'and those problem-solving puzzles. I'm good at classroom stuff, like science experiments and potions classes. I make a really good cup of tea,' he added as an afterthought.

'Hm,' replied Madame Demetria. 'Some of that might come in handy. But your physical fitness leaves a lot to be desired. How many sword fights have you ever won?'

'Zero.'

'Running races?'

'Zero.'

'Archery tournaments?'

'I won a contest once on a technicality.'

'Can you swim?'

'Yes! But not that quickly. Or with the best technique. I can stop myself from drowning,' he added defensively.

'Hm. Right, let's get you started with the basic assault course...'

By the time he had to get ready for school, all Richard had managed to do was clamber up, then fall off, a fifty-foot climbing wall that spewed boiling water. He re-joined Madame Demetria after lessons, and after three or five attempts he scaled the wall without slipping once and spent the rest of the evening trying to figure out how to climb down the other side.

The next morning, he ascended the wall on his first try, so Madame Demetria moved him on to sword practice, first with straw dummies and then with castle staff, who took bets on who would win each swordfight. Richard bet that the cook's seven-year-old daughter, a Princess Amelia fanatic who already owned her own sword, could beat him in less than ten seconds. He won the bet... and broke his glasses as he fell trying to escape his tiny opponent.

The day after that, they fit in the wall, sword work and animal tracking. A pattern formed: each morning saw the addition of a brutal, humiliating exercise designed to whip him into hero shape. Richard was just glad no one could record his training. The weeks became a blur of painful blunders and mortifying defeats in the sword fighting arena, on the obstacle course, and in lessons about how to distinguish between edible mushrooms, poisonous mushrooms and mushrooms that would make you think you were a seagull with rays of sunlight for eyeballs. Richard was never eating mushrooms again.

The only upside of being so busy was that the sinking feeling of doom that sat in the pit of Richard's stomach since he volunteered for his quest didn't get any bigger. Normally, anxiety built in Richard until he couldn't think of anything except the thing he was anxious about. When he wasn't training with Madame Demetria or cramming in schoolwork, he was so exhausted from climbing and fighting and studying that he couldn't seem to muster up any more feelings. He made a mental note to remember that for the future, if he ever came back.

Richard noticed an unexpected side effect of the training while dressing for a minor family engagement at a wine bar reopening. His trousers, which had always been comfortably tight, were hanging loose. He frowned and prodded his stomach. There was definitely less flab than he remembered. It was entirely possible he could feel muscles under there somewhere. As the least athletic member of the family, he had always been uncomfortable sitting for portraits next to his petite mother and wiry father. At school, his proudest achievement in a physical education lesson was staying upright during cross country. Now, as he trained as though his life depended on it—because his life *did* depend on it—he wasn't sure how to feel about his changing shape. He felt a little cross at himself for caring so much and went to find a belt.

After a particularly sweaty lesson in the arena about four weeks after he volunteered, Madame Demetria appraised Richard. She had a habit of picking her teeth with a pocketknife, so Richard found it hard to focus on her eye when she talked.

'You're ready.'

'Am I?'

'Well, no one's ever ready to face an evil magician. Or a mad prince. But your chances of not dying are now higher than your chances of dying.'

'Excellent.' Richard took a shaky breath. *Excellent.* Was he really doing this? He was really doing this. 'I'll leave tomorrow.'

The next day happened to be both the autumn equinox and Richard's fifteenth birthday, so that evening his parents threw a small going away-slash-birthday party for him. It may as well have taken place next to his headstone. Queen Florence cooked her legendary beef stew, but Richard was too busy trying not to think about statistics like *no one who has ever been to the tower on Ghost Mountain has come back* to taste it. At the end of the meal, Beatrice, who had been completely unfazed by their encounter with the Sapphire Dragon, presented him with her favourite teddy bear and a lightweight silver sword. 'Mrs Snuffles is so you can go to sleep properly,' she explained solemnly. 'And the sword is so you can stab yourself to death if it looks like you're going to be taken hostage by the Mad Prince.'

'It's so he can defend himself if he needs to,' Queen Florence corrected. 'Beatrice, what have I told you about reading Daddy's espionage books?'

Richard aimed for a laugh but made some sort of choking sound instead.

After dinner, when Beatrice was safely installed in bed with a picture book, King Richard called his son into his vast offices. A portrait of Helena, around the age Beatrice was now, hung above the fireplace. Richard always got a little chill when he recognised his own amber complexion and Beatrice's wonky smile. Her eyes, which were the same warm mahogany as Richard's, seemed to follow him around the room.

'How are you feeling?' the king asked carefully from across his enormous desk. He had Helena's eyes too.

Like I'm about to walk to my death, Richard wanted to reply. 'Nervous,' he said. 'I'm trying not to think too much about it. I just want to get to the Eaton estate in one piece, then reach the tower in one piece and then find whatever's in there. Then I'll think about getting me and him—it?— whatever's there—back to Laketown. In one piece. If it's even possible. If he—it—is real, or a spirit, or—'

'You'll do splendidly,' his father interrupted, but his smile did not quite erase the worry lines on his forehead. 'My coming-of-age quest was to travel down to the border with Kingdom of Mirrors and infiltrate a chess championship between the monarchies, to uncover a republican spy who was posing as a chess player. The spy was easy to find and deal with, of course, he was a terrible chess player—'

'But you met Mother there and she was much harder to charm.' Richard finished. The whole of the Three Kingdoms had heard this story dozens of times: it had been dramatised into four plays. Lady Florence, cousin to Queen Hazel, was the tournament's victor and a keen academic with no intention of marrying anyone. She refused to step out with Richard Senior until he proved he could speak four languages.

'Good night, Father. I'll see you in the morning.' Richard turned to leave.

'Wait, Richard, there's more. I—I have something for you.'

Aside from the eyes, King Richard didn't look much like his son. As well as Richard's being several shades darker, they held themselves differently: Richard Senior could shake a room's hand, but Richard Junior couldn't work out how to make the room pay attention when he was introduced. If you looked carefully, though, they had the same mannerisms. Both on edge, neither of them could stop tapping their foot to an imaginary beat. They weren't in time with each other. 'It's possible there's more than a mad priest or prince in that tower.'

'Several priests and princes?'

'No, a perfectly normal person who doesn't want to be disturbed.'

Richard nodded slowly. 'I did gather that it's unlikely to actually be anything supernatural.'

'Oh, good.' His father scratched his nose. 'Take these.' He thrust a pair of shoes into his son's hand. They were soft suede pumps, so thin they could have been stockings. 'For climbing the tower,' the King said. 'They're enchanted for extra sneakiness. Once you're wearing them, no one will hear you approach.'

Unfashionable *and* doomed to failure. How wonderful.

'Thank you, Father.' Richard wanted to ask if his father had any advice that didn't pertain to a chess competition twenty years ago, but he was already rifling through some paperwork: Richard was dismissed.

One of Richard's teachers once advised that if you found yourself disliking someone you should imagine them as a child, so Richard tried to imagine his father at his age, or even younger. Richard knew that in his twenties, Richard Senior was a dedicated, if headstrong, driving force behind the Valley of Dreams' state school system. In less than a decade he eradicated illiteracy and trebled the number of students accepted to university. He was also a celebrated scientist, working on crop yield and irrigation. Florence matched him in academic ability and softened his stubborn streak. Their daughter, Helena, shared the king's joy of reading and the queen's eye for chess games until she was killed in an accident on a school trip aged eight.

Try as he might, Richard could not conjure up an image of his father before his teenage years. He could never decide if that look of discomfort he wore around his children had been there before Helena died, or came after. Had he always preferred reading business papers to conversation?

With a sigh, Richard took one last look at Helena's portrait and returned to his room.

He was re-packing his bag when his mother knocked on his bedroom door.

'Come in,' he called, distracted. Queen Florence, already a head shorter than her son, stood in the doorway, watching him wrestle with his bag for several minutes before he threw it down in frustration.

'What's wrong?' she asked.

'It's just—' Richard couldn't say what he wanted to say because he didn't know what he wanted to say. *Help*, perhaps, or *how do I get rid of this feeling in my stomach that's making it hard to breathe?*

'Inhale and exhale for a count of ten,' his mother advised. 'Drink a glass of water. Lean into the feeling instead of ignoring it—that way it can't build up inside you.'

This was her advice for everything from a stubbed toe to a banking crisis and had been for as long as Richard could remember. He took a deep breath, exhaled and repeated it until his lungs were full. He prodded the dread in his stomach—what was he afraid of? Now he could breathe, it was obvious: the unknown. Trekking through his kingdom on his own. Being murdered by a bloodthirsty ghost magician. Being laughed at on his return and being told to hand his crown to Grant Westborough.

Why was his mother's advice always right?

'You're going to be fine,' she said gently, perching on the end of his bed. 'And if you aren't fine, well... at least you'll go out in a blaze of glory.'

Richard laughed in spite of himself. 'Mums are supposed to be adoring, not sarcastic!'

Florence smiled. 'There, I've made you laugh. Things can't be that bad.' She kissed his forehead and straightened his bedclothes. 'I'll make sure Bean gets walked twice a day.'

'Thanks. I'll—I'll try—' he didn't know how to say that he would try to make sure he didn't join Helena in the 'dead children of royals' history books.

Florence just smiled faintly and patted his hair. 'I know.'

Curled up next to Bean that night, Richard fell into dreams in which Grant threw him off an enormous cake stand into the jaws of a dragon.

Chapter Three

Richard awoke at first light feeling oddly empty. The soft silence of dawn usually settled his thoughts, but today his hands shook slightly as he pulled on two pairs of socks. Gods. No hero had ever worn two pairs of socks to prevent blisters. No hero studied sword fighting techniques in a book *before* trying them out, nor wore overlarge glasses. What was he doing?

Richard sat on the edge of his bed, forcing himself to focus on his breathing until he could no longer feel his heart constricting in his chest. He made himself focus on the worst possible outcome for this quest: death. Then he made himself think of the best possible outcome: survival with minimal injuries and mild respect from his peers. Acceptance from the kingdom that he was worthy of succeeding his father on the throne someday. The reality, he knew, was probably somewhere in the middle. The loss of a limb or two was likely, but so was discovery of the Mad Prince and a pat on the back from the king.

He took one last look at his bedroom, buried his head in Bean's fur for a moment, then headed to the courtyard to meet his parents. Florence tried to hide her distress, but she hugged him so fiercely he thought his ribs might crack.

As per quest rules, Richard had to find his own way north to the Eaton estate carrying nothing but his weapons, a small pouch of silver, some camping equipment and his books. Mrs Snuffles was tucked at the bottom of his pack next to a bar of emergency chocolate. Richard felt the same way about horses as he did heroes, so he elected to walk or hitchhike from Laketown to the Eaton estate, catching lifts on the back of wine carts or on boats along the Valley's complex canal system. At least no one would tell the press where he was going. As with all quests, the location and timeframe were to be kept publicly vague, so the young hero had to rely on their own wit and wisdom to fulfil it without outside help. That was the official line, anyway. The Eaton and Westborough families were more than happy to offer their sons a little extra assistance. Maybe all heroes secretly had their parents on standby.

Richard wondered if he was the first prince in centuries to take his quest alone.

The name Laketown was a misnomer: the city actually sat next to a lagoon. A century or so ago, someone with an eye for architecture added a pretty bridge allowing access from one end to the other. They installed a small statue dedicated to the people of the Valley at the bridge's centre, thus creating a tourist attraction. These days the lagoon was home to several migrating turtles, about one million fish and a mill that powered most of the infrastructure of Laketown. As he headed north out of the city, Richard tried not to think about the odds of never returning.

An unexpected downside to the quest: hours of alone time forced Richard to sit with his thoughts and analyse them with forensic precision. Now no one was watching, he could admit to himself that his main reason for swapping school and royal duties for smelly carts and possible dismemberment was jealousy of the other boys. *They* could all complete quests and swordfight properly... Richard had volunteered because he wanted people to look at him the way they did them. He consoled himself with the knowledge that, motives aside, he was embarking on his quest alone. No one was providing help, and he would succeed or fail on his own merits. That was something, wasn't it?

Richard slept in inns or his badly erected tent, hoping the wolf howls he could hear were in his imagination, and cooked food from his supplies. Gradually, once interest in his surroundings numbed the constant tug of anxiety, discomfort and hunger in his stomach, Richard realised that had never spent so much time exploring his own country. The family took day trips, of course, and often camped in the hills (usually with extra blankets and their servants nearby) but this was the first time Richard had ever travelled so extensively. He went days, sometimes, without speaking to a single person, but found himself occupied in every moment. He noticed that although the north of the Kingdom of Mirrors and the south of the Valley of Dreams were similar (hot, dry and stuffed with brightly-coloured buildings that could induce a major headache), the Valley had its own identity.

As he crept north, swirls and mosaics melted into square, pale stone buildings. Parakeets seemed quieter and better at flying in straight lines. Temples were dedicated to three or five gods, not twelve or twenty. Vineyards replaced olive trees. The Valley's great loves, wine and academia, were obvious in every village. Where there were people, there was a library and at least four inns, and every house had a table and chairs outside with little nooks for your wine glass and a book. There was also, Richard noted, a plethora of plant life. Even in built up areas, every home and garden held twenty or thirty trees or shrubs. Sometimes homeowners coordinated their gardens as though entering a contest: one housed nothing but roses in every colour while another contained fifteen different species of flower, every one bright orange. Here and there neighbours competed for the best display; Richard's favourite was a front garden with a fountain carved to look like a horse, right next to a garden with a shrub carefully groomed into the shape of a horse. The two stallions glared at each other over the picket fence.

This was what his 'getting back to nature' guidebook had talked about, but the text had not really conveyed the sense of inner peace Richard could feel even when forced to relieve himself behind a tree. Quietly, the Valley drew him in until he couldn't remember a time when he hadn't been totally in love with it.

Reaching the Stormhaven border from Laketown took several days longer than planned, mostly due to Richard taking accidental detours or needing to sit down while he nursed sore feet. He spent most evenings filling his pocketbook with notes and sketches of things he encountered. A one-legged lady in a village next to Charmedwater Canal who hopped around her garden, chasing her children with her wooden prosthetic; an entire village of Kingdom of Mirrors refugees near the Valley University of Spells and Enchantments, whose homes were covered in painted tiles and mosaiced glass chips; a strange town Richard couldn't find on a map, where chimneys released pink smoke and watering cans bobbed along in mid-air. Without his family crest on his clothes, nobody seemed to recognise that Richard was royalty and he was glad for the peace and quiet.

As Richard edged closer to the Stormhaven border, he noticed several families coming the other way, laden with suitcases and heavy bags. A few had carts or horses, but most walked. He counted nine families over three days, one with twelve people who looked like they spanned four or five generations. The oldest member of the group, a wizened old lady perched on a donkey, held a tiny newborn. Richard remembered Princess Amelia asking him about northern refugees: was this what she was talking about? Were these people fleeing Stormhaven? He liked the Kingdom of Mirrors, but he couldn't imagine why anyone would voluntarily move there from somewhere as affluent as Stormhaven.

Richard eventually started noticing signs of the vast Eaton estate. Banners advertised amenities: *Try the best wine in the Valley, good times or your money back! Value your magical items at the Emporium for Magical Antiquities, no. 11 Vine Street. FRUIT PICKERS WANTED: APPLY AT MIRASOL'S INN.*

So, too, Richard saw the dregs of a society built on alcohol: an unkempt man who could have been anywhere between twenty and fifty, slumped on the path. Richard debated what he should do: on the one hand, no one passed out on an open road in broad daylight could be said to be living their best life. On the other, drunk people were unpredictable until you found out which type of drunk they were.

His decision was made before he reached the vagrant: a couple of teenagers Richard's age who were passing the other way stopped and scooped up stones from the roadside. 'Hey!' Richard called. 'Don't—'

One stone hit the man in his side. Another hit him in the leg.

He sat up, groggy, as a third stone glanced off his head, leaving a slick red line.

'Hey!' Richard ran forward. 'Leave him alone!' The boys, who were younger and weaker jawed up close, sniggered but hurried away.

'Are you okay? Richard asked, already digging in his bag for medical supplies. 'Here, have some tonic—'

The man was gone.

Richard saw no sign of him on the road, although he kept his first aid kit handy just in case.

The sun was low in the sky by the time Richard set foot on the Eaton estate proper. In front of him stretched miles of vineyards, an enormous mansion and a little village tacked on as an afterthought. Ghost Mountain loomed over the valley, green and picturesque except for the silhouette of a ruined tower at the very top. Just beyond the Eaton estate was the border with Stormhaven, marked by a small fence and a few signs. Dozens more mountains were hazy in the distance.

If Richard hadn't known he was likely facing a painful death, he would have considered himself fortunate to have travelled all this way through the best landscape in the Three Kingdoms. As it was, he sealed his pocketbook into an addressed envelope and dropped it into a post box, so his family would know that the quest wasn't a total waste of time, even if it did kill him. Then he double-checked Mrs Snuffles was secure and strode into the village.

By now it was fully autumn but still warm, so Richard stopped at Mirasol's Inn for dinner before climbing the mountain. He was nervous about approaching the tower at twilight, but he wanted to reserve the element of surprise... plus it would be easier to hide in the dark if his nerves got the better of him.

'You're a bit young to be questing up to the tower by yourself, aren't you?' Mirasol, a tiny lady with sunflowers in her hair, inspected him closely when she took his order.

'I won't actually be going there,' Richard lied, 'I'm a history student. I'm here to use the library for a school project about the haunted tower.'

'It's haunted all right,' she said grimly, as though she hadn't even heard the bit about history, 'but not by ghosts.' Richard tried to look nonchalant.

'Really? You think someone lives there?'

'Oh yes. Ghosts don't cause strobe lights to go off in the middle of the night, and they don't steal food.'

'Food?'

Mirasol leaned in. 'Every villager's noticed it. Once every few weeks, one of us has something stolen. Some vegetables and grains, a jar of olives or smoked meat. We've had a hog roast nicked right off the spit.'

'That does seem unusual for a ghost,' Richard agreed. 'Have you ever noticed anything else?' A thought occurred to him. 'Nothing else has been stolen, has it?'

'Well...' Mirasol glanced at the inn's only other guest, an elderly man munching his way through a steak. 'Don't go advertising this, but my sister-in-law works at the tailors. She told me a few years ago that they came to work one day to find the loom gone.'

'Hm.'

'And the big house with the vineyards, the Eaton mansion; they once had a toilet stolen.'

Richard inhaled his glass of water. 'A toilet? How do you know?'

'My daughter Nina works there. Old Lord Eaton isn't very popular with his staff, so she quite enjoyed seeing him complain about it. Apparently, there are four bathrooms in that mansion, but the thief vandalised his favourite.'

'How unusual.'

'I know,' Mirasol agreed. 'Who would have a favourite toilet?'

Chapter Four

Richard made for the mountain after dinner, taking care not to be seen by locals who might get it in their minds to stop him or, worse, come along too. Ghost Mountain was not the tallest mountain in the Three Kingdoms by a long stretch, but years of infamy made it steeper and less forgiving of visitors. Glaring down at him from the summit was an ancient, depressingly evil-looking stone tower.

It took the best part of two hours to reach the peak, by which time Richard was drenched in sweat and sure his dislike of horses was one of those things he should have tried harder to get over. The path was relatively well-worn but the sun, even as it set, was unforgiving. He was painfully aware that anyone watching from the tower would probably see approaching visitors, which might explain why so few knights or lords had defeated whatever lived there.

As Richard caught his breath in the shadow of a cypress tree and took in his surroundings, he realised two things. The first was that the building in front of him was nothing like the tower he had glimpsed on the ascent. Instead of the typical curved towers and pale, ornate walls of Valley architecture, this three-story building was rectangular, symmetrical and blocky. What's more, this building was *new*. The courtyard was polished, the windows held all their panes. There were even signs of decoration: flagstones arranged in a pattern, curtains in the windows. Then there was the date, lovingly carved into the stone above a large, latticed door: midsummer, two years previously. This house was finished two years before Richard arrived. But how? All that was visible from the ground was the one enormous, dilapidated stone tower.

The hairs on the back of Richard's neck stood up. Where *was* the tower? This place was beautiful, but there wasn't a tower in sight.

There was really nothing left but to go in. As Richard picked up his bag, a movement caught the corner of his eye. At first he thought it might be a dragon and reached for his weapons. Madame Demetria's lessons seemed very far away. Then the building swayed. Richard paused, hand hovering above his sword. Buildings did not sway, even magical ones. Richard blinked and pinched himself. The building was still swaying. Then it crackled, like a ripple through water. Its walls fell inwards, silently crumbling, like the earth was pulling it in. Within a moment the entire structure was gone.

In its place stood a malicious architect's masterpiece, a looming tower with one hundred little windows, reaching up to the clouds. Mossy stone gargoyles leered down as ravens shrieked overhead. The whole building seemed to be weeping: in some places, water ran down the walls. In others, blood. Bones littered the ground near it, from small bird skeletons to what looked worryingly like a human spine.

What a place to call home. Richard scanned the tower until he saw an enormous wooden door, its handle carved into the shape of a skull. It would have looked at home in the Laketown prison. He took a breath and started toward it—

Wait—his shoes. Richard pulled off his hiking boots and tugged on the suede pumps. They looked like beige ballet shoes. He tapped a foot experimentally. He couldn't hear it hit the ground. He jumped up and down, then ran to the tower door. Nothing. Maybe this prince would have fewer eyes than Madame Demetria and all Richard would need to do was sneak up on him. It was a comforting thought.

Richard turned the door handle experimentally.

Of course it was open.

A steep stone staircase greeted him. There was no bannister and no light except from the tiny windows. The inside walls were weeping too. Richard took one last look at the sky and started climbing.

The journey was not fun. In fact, Richard preferred hiking up the mountain. At least the mountain had things to look at. This staircase just went on, in an upwards circle, until Richard had forgotten why he started climbing in the first place. The only way he knew time was passing was that sometimes he heard birds calling to each other far below and noticed the light change as it filtered through the windows. Sometimes he thought he could hear footsteps far above him, or maybe far below. Sometimes he thought he could hear crying—or was it laughter? The entire building smelt vaguely of animal, like the rabbit hutch at the castle.

Richard wondered what they were all doing back home and promptly felt so homesick he had to stop for a moment. Beatrice had been nursing a wobbly tooth when he left. Maybe it had fallen out, or maybe she was conspiring to tie a string to the offending tooth and slam a door, which was what she had done with three previous loose teeth despite the concerted efforts of everyone in the household. Were his parents well? Were they thinking of him? Were they wondering what it might be like to lose another child? Richard was born two years to the day after Helena's death, and despite all expectations did not remotely live up to his older sister's legacy. The king and queen obviously loved their son very much (and followed his arrival with a third child just in case another accident should occur), but Richard could never shake the feeling that they couldn't look at his achievements without wondering how Helena could have done in the same circumstances. Then again, Richard had relatively few achievements.

This *tower*. It was eating his brain. Or maybe those feelings were there all the time and he only acknowledged them because he was too far from civilisation for anyone to see him sniffling into his sleeve.

He took a few more steps, then a few more. His legs burned. Just when he really thought he might be here forever—

Another huge door. No embellishments or fancy locks. Just standard and wooden with a heavy iron doorknob. It was ajar.

Richard drew his sword, took a deep breath and prodded the door. It was heavy, but barely made a sound as it swung open a smidgeon, just enough that Richard could poke his head around it.

The Prince in the Tower

Chapter Five

Well.

This was anticlimactic.

A single, plush armchair was pulled close to a little fire, crackling merrily in an enormous fireplace. Curled in the chair was a—a teenage boy?

No, a man. The firelight cast odd shadows against his face; his skin looked like stone. He couldn't be a child—nobody that young could look that ancient. He was reading a book. In fact, he was so absorbed that he did not seem to have noticed the door open. A small part of Richard's brain was surprised about the book. An even smaller part of his brain was surprised he was surprised about the book. Surely even mad magical banished princes and/or priests and/or evil ghosts were allowed books.

Emboldened, Richard padded into the room and stared around. The chamber was completely circular, with sweeping wall tapestries depicting dragons and unicorns and legendary epic battles. Several large windows, currently covered by rich velvet curtains, would probably have afforded the best views in the Valley. One or two wall lamps cast a cosy glow across a neatly made four poster bed, blankets folded carefully. Shiny calf-high leather boots were propped next to a small wardrobe. A loom sat next to one of the windows; a large pot plant sat next to another. A silver teapot perched on a wooden table next to a china cup. Several shelves were lined with the sort of books you only saw in libraries: enormous, leather-bound and embossed with gold leaf. One window must have been left open: Richard could smell fresh air.

This was all rather warmer and more comfortable than Richard had expected. It was also distinctly… fancier.

He turned his attention to the figure in the chair. He wore clothes smarter than Richard would have expected—excellently tailored and very modern. A rich black jumper, soft trousers and thick socks. He was also very clean, which struck Richard as odd. How many insane-prisoner-magicians washed regularly? Was this tower even connected to the water system? The thought of someone lugging Lord Eaton's toilet all the way up the stairs was so ridiculous that Richard almost laughed. He took another deep breath to steady himself.

Because this was not the villain's lair Richard had imagined, he retreated a few steps back to the entrance and knocked.

The man jumped. No, Richard was right first time: the *boy* jumped. He was definitely a teenager, now he had moved. He recovered quickly, blinking, and pulled his eyes back to his book: a huge, well-worn volume that needed both hands to hold upright.

'Er, hello,' Richard said.

'Welcome to my tower, hero,' the boy replied. He had very straight teeth. 'I normally get up to greet visitors, but I'm at a really good bit.' Richard glanced at the cover: *Insights into the Kingdom Wars*.

'The author does a good job of explaining the Clan Wars, but he completely missed out the significance of the Housewives' Revolt. If you want to get a good idea of what actually brought the wars to a close, you really need to read Professor Tiffany Marinos' book *Women and the Household in the Kingdom Wars*. The second edition is better.' Richard heard himself speak but wasn't sure what had prompted him to do so. What was he doing? This was not a history lesson. Richard bit his lip. Madame Demetria hadn't really suggested what to do if the Mad Prince appeared to be a bookworm.

The boy finally looked towards Richard. His eyes were blue, the sort of blue you associate with frostbitten limbs and hypothermia, his hair was silver blonde. He was tall and skinny, too, all folded over in his chair, with a square face and a chalky pallor: nothing like the short, stocky, olive-skinned locals down in the Valley.

He yawned and shrugged, like complete strangers walked into his home and started talking about academic texts all the time. 'If you say so. Would you like a drink?'

'Ex-excuse me?'

'A drink. I'm having one. Not on your account—I always have one in the evening—but as you're here…'

Richard could hear his mother's lectures about underage drinking and taking food from strangers, but he could also hear her instructions to always accept hospitality from your host. This host was wearing a dagger on his belt and could make buildings disappear, so Richard nodded.

The boy clicked his fingers and a second armchair appeared across from his own. He clicked them again and a drinks trolley laden with cut glass bottles appeared between the chairs. He poured two glasses of what looked suspiciously like brandy. How very grown-up. Maybe he was actually eighty-five and had discovered a really good anti-ageing potion but got into trouble because he wouldn't give the recipe to Queen Margaret.

'Sit down,' the boy snapped as he secured the top on the brandy bottle. 'You're making me anxious.' Richard almost laughed again.

'Is the chair trapped?'

'What? No. I wasn't thinking that far ahead when I conjured it. Just sit before I turn you into a frog.'

Richard didn't put his sword down, but he perched on the edge of the chair. It was ridiculously comfortable. Maybe that was the trap. He accepted the glass the boy was holding out but didn't raise it to his mouth until the boy had taken a drink. He sniffed it and couldn't detect alcohol or deadly poison, not that he would necessarily have been able to. He took a reluctant sip and his throat burned: it was nothing like brandy and everything like molten vanilla ice cream. Richard finally understood why vanilla was a spice.

Richard put the glass down and gripped his sword, frantically trying to remember if his warrior classes had said anything about handsome magicians with non-alcoholic liqueur collections, and if so, what the protocol was. He wished he could remember the way out of the tower and back down the mountain in total darkness. Clearly, this boy was neither a crazy old priest nor a ghost. Why would a child magician be living in an old tower?

'What's your name?' Richard asked.

'George.'

'Nice to meet you, George.'

'You don't mean that,' the boy replied with a smirk.

'No, I don't mean it,' Richard admitted. Old stories fluttered around Richard's brain, cancelling one another out until he could only think of one that fit the facts. 'Are you... are you a prince?'

'Yes.' The boy seemed startled. 'Of course. Don't *you* know who I am?'

'Er, no. Never heard of a Prince George.'

'My name isn't in your history books?'

'Nope.' Richard glanced at *Insights into the Kingdom Wars*. 'And I've read *a lot* of history books.'

'Oh.' He sounded like Alistaire or one of the boys at school: petulant and put out that he wasn't more appreciated.

It dawned on Richard that he wasn't feeling very scared anymore. It was possible his brain had reached its maximum daily capacity for fear and simply couldn't process any more, but it was also possible that the feeling in the pit of Richard's stomach was irritation. After days of walking, hours of climbing, years of psyching himself up to volunteer on a quest, he may as well have been back at a garden party. The prince in the tower was just a boy, in a lavish armchair, who thought people should know his name but hadn't asked Richard his.

Richard stood up and levelled his sword at the prince's head.

'George—can I call you George?'

'No.'

'George, if you're going to kill me, could you please just get it over with? I'm Richard, by the way,' Richard added as an afterthought. 'If you're going to murder me and leave my bones at your front door, you should probably know my name.'

The boy blinked.

'Ex-excuse me?'

'Just get it over with,' Richard repeated. 'Please.'

A flicker of confusion crossed his face. 'Most people... Most heroes beg me to spare their life.'

'Well, clearly I am not a hero.' Richard felt oddly impatient. 'So get on with it.'

A moment ticked by, then another. Then another. The boy blinked several times. Richard waited.

'I... I can't.'

'Can't spare my life or can't kill me?' Richard felt as though he were back at the obstacle course.

'I...' The prince's eyes were watering a bit. For the first time, Richard got the impression that he and this boy might be the same age. 'I won't kill you. I never kill them.'

'Oh.' Well, that was a nice surprise. 'Then how...' Richard looked around the room. 'Do you keep everyone prisoner here?' The prince said nothing, but he picked at a thumbnail until it started to bleed. His eyes were suspiciously shiny.

Richard thought of the journey upstairs, the animal smell. *Sit before I turn you into a frog.*

'You don't kill your assailants,' Richard realised. 'You transform them... into animals?'

'Yes, fine,' the prince snapped, a pink flush splashing across his face. 'I transfigure them.' He sniffed. 'This is hay fever, obviously.'

'Take a deep breath ten times,' Richard suggested. 'In through the nose, out through the mouth. Drink some water. Lean into your—lean into whatever you're feeling. That way it—hay fever—can't build up.'

The prince took a ragged breath. Richard put his sword back on his belt and looked out of the window. He counted ten breaths of his own, then ten more.

Richard glanced over sporadically. Several seconds ticked by in which the prince tried to look very much like he wasn't reaching for a handkerchief.

'Would you like a cup of tea and some chocolate?' Richard asked after the prince had blown his nose.

'Pardon?'

'Tea and chocolate. I'm having some. I always do when I've had a traumatic evening in a magician's tower. I noticed the kettle on your table, so…'

'Er, go ahead.' The prince blinked. 'There's milk in that cupboard.'

'Do you take sugar?'

'Er, no.'

Richard set the kettle over the fire and discovered a spare cup on a shelf. Next to a jug of milk in the stone ice cupboard sat a tiny wheel of cheese and a minuscule jar of jam.

Once the tea was brewed and poured, Richard dug into his backpack and fished out his emergency chocolate. He applied his mother's homemade magical hand cleaner, then broke the bar in two. He held out the larger part to the prince, who took it. Both their fingers were shaking a bit.

'Thank you.' His voice sounded a bit rusty.

Richard plopped down on the floor with his teacup, sat cross-legged, and took a bite out of his chocolate. After a moment's hesitation George joined him.

'Um, is that a teddy bear?' Something had fallen from Richard's pack; he scooped it up gently.

'That's Mrs Snuffles.'

'Mrs Snuffles?'

'My sister gave her to me. Be careful, she's insured for more than I am.' He tucked the bear back into his bag and returned to his chocolate. They were quiet for a moment. Richard was always taught that it was rude to stare at people while they ate, so he gazed around the room instead. It was the sort of neat you only achieve when you have too much time on your hands.

'So, Prince George.' Richard tested his name. 'What's the real story of the magician in the tower? Do you just transfigure everyone who comes here?'

'Yes. Usually into cats.'

'Cats.'

'I either set them loose or give them to people down in the village. Well. I might have kept one or two.' Richard would never look at a household pet in the same way again.

'Can you show me a magic trick?' Richard asked, despite himself.

George held out his hand. A yellow flame appeared, winding itself together into a knot. The knot performed a small jive, unwound itself then danced through the air and right out the door. It was incredibly cool, but Richard wasn't going to tell him that.

George appeared to be watching the fire as he sipped tea, but every so often Richard noticed his eyes glance toward him, like he was trying to figure out what to do with his visitor.

'So, Prince Richard,' George said eventually. 'What's the real story of the prince on the quest?'

'This is my coming-of-age quest,' Richard said. 'I was supposed to... hang on. How do you know I'm a prince?'

'Your name is Richard,' George pointed out, 'and the papers are full of Prince Richard de la Fuente's recent decision to quest to an unknown location.'

'Oh.' Richard felt mildly embarrassed that the rest of the kingdom was following his exploits over their breakfast. That this stone-carved magician was reading along too made Richard feel oddly undone.

'So,' continued George, unaware of Richard's discomfort, 'your quest was to murder me and haul my corpse back to the castle?'

'Well. Sort of. No. Ideally I'm to bring you back to Laketown. The Eatons will want compensation for the trouble on their estate.'

'Oh, the Eatons. What a lovely family. I must thank them for the use of their bathroom fixtures.' Richard couldn't see any doors off this room except the one he'd entered by, so he decided not to ask the location of the lavatory.

A thought occurred to Richard. 'How old are you?'

'Fourteen. Fifteen. I can't—I can't remember exactly.'

'How long have you been living in the tower?'

'Since I was eight.'

'You've been in this room since you were eight. Would you like to elaborate on how you got here?'

'Not really, no.'

'Were you left here by accident, imprisoned or abandoned?'

A scowl crossed George's face. 'Let's go with *abandoned*.' He did not look ready to elaborate on that, either.

'Okay. But how are you not…' Richard paused.

'Insane?' George smirked over his teacup. 'Who's to say I haven't gone insane?'

'I was going to say *traumatised*. You're wearing the latest fashions and you're speaking with the same accent as the locals. There is no way you have spent the last seven years alone in this room.'

George reached into his pocket and pulled out a small glass vial. He tapped the contents into his palm—some kind of tincture or potion—then splashed it onto his face. Blue smoke engulfed him, and Richard coughed. The air smelt like sawdust and grease.

The smoke cleared and the vagrant from earlier was sat on the floor. Same curly red hair, rough skin, brown eyes. Short, grubby, nothing like Prince George.

'See?' George shrugged. His voice was scratchier too, like he had spent three decades smoking. 'It's easy to slip into the world and back out of it again when you know how.'

Richard blinked. Now he knew he was looking at an illusion, the seams were obvious. The vagrant's eyes were blueish brown, the dirt on his face didn't seem to move with his muscles and there were tinges of blonde in that reddish hair. George splashed more tincture on his face and melted into the elderly man at the inn, earlier.

'I probably get out the house more than you do,' he said, voice now raspy and worn out, but there was no malice in his tone. Deep lines were etched across his face, his shoulders were hunched and his hair was grey and wispy. He looked older than most old people. George flicked another drop of potion on to his face and within ten seconds, his appearance was his own. Up close, he was the sort of handsome that makes you say 'oh, that mountain lion is handsome!' right before it bites your head off. There were little silver flecks amongst all the blue in his eyes, and Richard noticed the stone from earlier had left a tidy scratch on the side of his head. He fought a momentary urge to touch it.

'Why me? I mean, why wait for me on the road?' Richard pulled himself back to the present with the realisation that George hadn't asked his name because he hadn't needed to. 'And I don't get the impression that you personally greet every one of your visitors with a drink before you turn them into an animal. Also, why did you play the trick with the building?'

'I always do the trick with the building. It makes people anxious.' Richard didn't like to mention that the dripping, shrieking tower was pretty anxiety-inducing by itself. George continued, oblivious, 'I waited on the road because I wanted to see if you are like all the others. I wasn't sure if you would come to my tower on your quest, but I wanted to keep my eye out in case I should prepare for battle.'

'And what did you learn?'

George did not meet his eyes. 'I did not expect you to help me with those boys. Or to sneak up on me in your magic shoes. Or to have read a book on the Clan Wars.'

'We are definitely the only two people in the Three Kingdoms to have read that book,' Richard admitted. A small smile appeared near George's mouth.

A sound made Richard jump—he reached for his sword as the door creaked and through it crept—

'Is that—is that a kitten?'

A small tabby cat plodded over to George and sat in his lap.

'This is—er, a knight from Stormhaven. He tried climbing the tower a few months ago.'

Richard studied the cat. 'I have a feeling my father would know you.'

'So, you came here on your coming-of-age quest. Why now? You don't have to do it until you're sixteen or so. Surely your father could pull some strings to avoid you ever having to do it, since you're literally royalty...'

The thought of asking King Richard for a reprieve from his duties was so laughable it had never actually occurred to Richard. 'I just—I just got fed up with people implying that I didn't deserve to be next in line to the throne because I'm not—not very princely. So I volunteered to come up here, just to make the point that I could.' It sounded even more embarrassing out loud. 'It was stupid.'

'I don't think you're stupid. I've read about the rumours surrounding Ghost Mountain. I think you're brave.'

Richard let the compliment wash over him as the kitten got up, stretched and wandered to where he sat. He held out his hand and the kitten permitted him to scratch it behind the ear.

Why would anyone have put George in this tower? No one in the Valley of Dreams would carry out such a barbaric act against a child—especially not to a prince. Just how senior a royal was he? If he'd been abandoned by Queen Margaret, why did he change his appearance to leave the tower? Unless he'd been imprisoned and didn't want anyone to know he was perfectly capable of walking down the mountain and off the estate?

All these questions seemed to Richard as though they would ruin the friendly atmosphere, so he just asked, 'Why don't you leave? There's nothing stopping you, especially in a disguise.'

George gazed at the fire. 'Even with a potion, that sort of magic takes concentration. I can't do it for long, and I always cast a protection charm to stop people from focusing on the details. It's a lot of work. But a disguise is a good way to get out and about… I'm in a football team,' he added unexpectedly. He didn't look strong enough to run the length of a pitch. 'I went to the local school too, for a few years… until I sat my final year tests and they figured out there were no records of me.'

Richard looked at George with renewed respect. Would he, if left to live in a terrifyingly bleak tower completely alone, have the integrity to join the local school?

'I suppose I could go. I walked halfway to Charmedwater Canal once.' Now he was talking, George seemed almost unable to stop. How long was it since he had a proper conversation with someone his own age? 'I could even wear my own face, it's been ages since they—I've been here ages now. But I have nowhere to go. Almost no one who comes up here has heard of me. I assumed you'd know who I am because I was a—I know that royal children are usually taught the names of everyone in the Three Kingdoms' royal families. I checked newspaper records in the village once, but there was nothing about my being left here.' He swallowed. 'No one's ever come to look for me.'

Richard thought for a moment. He still had dozens of questions but didn't want to push his luck. 'You should come back to Laketown with me. Not as a prisoner.'

'Why?'

'My parents should know that a supposedly haunted tower is actually harbouring an abandoned royal child. Besides, I have to bring back proof I've rid the tower of the ghost or no one will believe me.'

George looked about to respond when a tiny bell on the bedside cabinet rang of its own accord, emitting a purple light. Fear gripped Richard—had he walked into a trap after all?—but before he could grab his sword, George murmured, 'Intruder alarm.'

Richard sat up, gently manoeuvring the kitten off his lap. It scampered to a cushion. George closed his eyes briefly and clapped. A misty hologram appeared in the air in front of them, showing the entrance to the tower and a cloaked figure clad in armour. The air rippled and Richard realised the newcomer was seeing the illusion of the modern castle melt away. After a moment's hesitation, the figure stepped forward and through the huge tower door, which Richard had left open in case he needed to leave in a hurry.

'Two visitors in an evening. I'm honoured.' George looked old again, in sudden stark contrast to his expression before. This, Richard realised, was a normal day for him.

'How long do we have before they get here?' Richard asked.

'Maybe five minutes.'

'Five—wait, how long did it take me to get here?'

'About forty minutes. I cast a spell on the stairs to make them seem longer and scare people, so I'd have time to prepare to meet them, but I'm already paying attention, so—hang on, let me take it off—' he snapped his fingers and pulled a face. 'It took me ages to perfect the sound effects.'

'We should set a trap for them.' Richard said suddenly. 'Before you turn them into a cat. Maybe no one's heard of you because you aren't asking the right questions.' George raised an eyebrow.

'Are you any good at traps?'

'Not usually, but—I have an idea.'

Four minutes and thirty seconds later, the door pushed open and a hooded figure slunk into the room. George was sitting in his armchair, his eyes on his book. The kitten sat in the corner, watching intently.

'Arise, foul creature!' the hooded person shouted, lurching toward George, who made a wonderful show of jumping up and grabbing his dagger.

'Bow before me, magician, and tell me where you've put the prince!' the intruder snapped. He raised his sword—as Richard stepped forward and threw a net over him. Quick as lightning, George threw gold dust over the net and it sealed itself. The intruder stumbled and fell in a little pool of material.

'Hey! Ow!'

Oh gods. Richard *knew* that voice. Mortification ran through him like he had swallowed hot tea too quickly. Couldn't he have one quest to himself? Just one?

He stepped forward, reached through the net and tugged the hood from the person's head.

'You!' the intruder snapped. 'Let me out of this net!'

Richard sighed. 'Hello, Alistaire.'

'Wait…' George frowned. 'You know this boy?'

Richard nodded. 'His name is Alistaire. With an extra E. He's, um, someone I go to school with. His dad owns the estate down the mountain. Lord Eaton.'

'I'm also a hero!' Alistaire called through the net. Richard noticed, with a sinking feeling, that Alistaire was not wearing his family's crest of a gold grape vine on a green backdrop. On his armour was the coat of arms of the House of Stars, a star and fish design.

'Why are you here, Alistaire? Why did you ask George where I was?'

'I wanted to stop you from hurting yourself! Everyone knew you would be terrible at your quest!'

Forget Richard's earlier discomfort. *This* was mortification. He would be the first hero to die of embarrassment. *He was actually melting in a blaze of humiliation.*

'Someone sent you... to rescue Prince Richard from me?' George asked. Richard couldn't look at him.

'Before you killed him, yes.'

'Well, this is awkward,' George said. 'Because I'm going to kill *you*.'

'What?' Richard asked.

'What?' Alistaire asked.

'Well, we were having quite a nice evening,' George explained, 'and you've ruined it by breaking into my tower and trying to attack me. Bit rude.' *Quite a nice evening.* Was it? Maybe.

Alistaire seemed to notice for the first time that Richard and George were standing next to each other. He looked as though he was doing some very quick thinking, which was a new expression for him. 'You should stay in here, Richard, and let me sort out the prince outside. I'm here to help you!'

'Alistaire why would you want to help me? No offence, but you've always come across as someone who thinks I'd be better off out of your way.'

Alistaire blinked 'I didn't... I was told...' he seemed to be waiting for them to free him. When neither of them did, he continued, snippily, 'this is not my first ever quest. I defeated a chimera once. Let me deal with this maniac outside!' Richard rolled his eyes.

They waited, but Alistaire seemed to have dried up.

Richard could smell a rat, and it wasn't Alistaire.

'You know what, Alistaire, I don't think George is as bad as people have been saying.' Richard decided not to mention that when George said 'kill' he meant 'turn you into a small mammal.' He rather thought Alistaire would make a good weasel. 'I think he's just quite private. Is that accurate?' He glanced at George, who nodded.

'It's a nightmare, dealing with knights and lordlings who need to put your head on a spike to prove themselves. Did you know, Adrian, that your friend was the first person to talk about books with me? In seven years? It's all questing for glorious bloodshed with these people. Can you blame me for putting up a few home security systems?'

Alistaire looked as though he were about to agree, then changed his mind and scowled at them through the net. 'Who told you to follow me?' Richard asked.

'Your father! He told me he couldn't bear to lose another child and he'd do anything to make sure you returned safely, even if it meant ruining your quest.' That did not sound like the distant, respectful man with whom Richard had last spoken. In the de la Fuente family, you stood or fell on your own abilities.

'If my father sent you, why are you wearing the badge of the Kingdom of Mirrors? Why are you trying to get me to stay in this room?'

Alistaire blinked again. Richard peered at him. He looked fully miserable, his normally shiny black curls matted and dirty, his cloak torn. On his last quest he probably had minions to patch him up and make sure he washed his hair regularly. 'I'm not allowed to tell you.'

George was looking carefully at Alistaire and Richard, as if weighing up whether to speak. 'Richard, I think we should go to Laketown immediately. With Adrian.'

Richard blinked. The casual use of 'we' caught him off guard. 'Why? Do you... do you know something about this? Whatever *this* is...'

George looked uncomfortable. 'Maybe. Possibly. I don't—I don't know.' He looked back at Alistaire and something like guilt crossed his face for a split second. Then he clicked his fingers, and before Richard could blink, a small brown rabbit sat in the net where Alistaire had been.

'What did you do that for—' before Richard could finish his sentence, George had clicked his fingers again, produced a little wooden carry case from thin air and bundled the rabbit out of the net and into the case.

'He'll be fine,' George said as Richard gaped. 'There's food and water in there.'

'What was that—'

'Look, I didn't want to say in front of him, but I think his family's up to something.' He took a deep breath, looking more uncomfortable than he had at any point in the last hour. 'It could be nothing, but when I go out in the village, I often overhear things. Usually it's just gossip, but... a few times Lord Eaton's been spotted with some of the other lords going in and out of his mansion. According to staff, they've been having meetings and it looks like they don't want anyone to hear them, because they had the best magician in the village cast silencing spells on his study. But it's not just that. Some of the lords have been wearing Stormhaven crests. The Queen's coat of arms.'

'Are you sure?'

'I had a look for myself after I heard the rumours. I—I recognised some of the lords.' Definitely one of Margaret's nephews, then.

Richard's head was spinning. His father's High Council was full of old, beardy aristocrats who owned about five hundred vineyards between them and liked nothing better than to complain about the influx of southern refugees. They were all snobby and crotchety, and Lord Eaton the snobbiest and crotchetiest, but none of them had ever struck Richard as particularly nefarious.

Richard gazed at the fire. Why was Alistaire so insistent that Richard stay in the tower? He thought about *Insights into the Kingdom Wars*. Historically, lords meeting under cover did not mean anything good for the monarchy. It usually meant the kingdom was in for a spate of kidnappings and attempted coups and—

Kidnappings.

'George, could you turn Alistaire back into a person for a moment, please?'

George shrugged and pulled the wriggling rabbit from the case. He clicked his fingers and there was Alistaire, even more dishevelled.

'What was that—'

'Alistaire, your father has sent you to lock me in this tower while he stages a coup against my father, hasn't he? He's going to blame my kidnap on the Durante family, or Prince George, or both.'

Alistaire gaped. 'How… how did you know that?'

'I didn't until you just told me.'

George looked like he was trying not to smile as he clicked his fingers. Alistaire disappeared. The rabbit looked up at them as if to say, *I hope you both get fleas.*

Richard looked down at the rabbit for a minute. He wanted a cup of tea while he thought about what Alistaire had been trying to do, but he knew he should—they should—make for Laketown immediately. How long could rabbits be kept in cages?

'George, can you conjure me a lead for the rabbit?'

'A lead?'

'Yes, a lead. With a collar. So we can let him out of the cage without him running away.'

'Oh. Good idea.' Another click of George's fingers and the rabbit was wearing some sort of harness. Beatrice would have fallen in love with him.

Richard took his glasses off and cleaned them on his shirt. When he'd pictured this part of the quest, he'd imagined the prince in chains, or knocked unconscious from a sword fight. He had not imagined walking down the tower stairs with George as an ally. They *had* passed a pleasant evening, after the almost-being-turned-into-an-animal bit and before the weird kidnap attempt. 'Right. Let's go to Laketown. After I've changed my shoes and figured out where your bathroom is. Wait—can you even get down the mountain safely in the dark?'

'Of course you can,' George said briskly, striding round the room and stuffing objects into a leather holdall. 'Just ask a magician.'

Chapter Six

Richard felt the journey down the mountain was easier for having someone to guide him, but harder for having possession of live cargo. George threw dust into the air as they stood at the tower's front door, which lit the sky in pale yellow light and dispersed down the mountain, tracing a path. Just before they set off, George looked back up at the tower. A look of trepidation crossed his face. Richard wondered how he felt about leaving, and whether he planned to come back. Before they descended the stairs, he tidied everything away, taking the perishable food and the pot plant with them, collecting every cat he could find and locking the door carefully behind them.

'Will you wear a disguise?' Richard asked. George shrugged. He was levitating the animal cages so they could leave their hands free and had provided Richard with an old oil lamp. Richard wondered how George felt at having made a new acquaintance. A friend, even. Richard, for his part, could not remember the last time he made a new friend.

'No one in the village knows my real face… but I suppose there's no point breaking the habit of a lifetime.' George sprinkled some potion onto his face and hands. His white blonde hair turned coppery brown, his skin the same amber hue as Richard's. 'We should stop once we're down the mountain, though, so I can reapply it.'

They didn't talk much on the descent, and Richard led the way through the village to Mirasol's Inn. He glanced at the clock in the village square and realised he had only been gone about six hours—it was just past midnight.

Mirasol greeted him enthusiastically as they walked through the door. 'You enjoyed your little evening jaunt up the tower, then? Did you learn lots of history? Did you kill the prince?' Richard could *feel* George's hostility.

'I'm only here for a school project. May my friend and I eat here?'

'Of course. You'll have to put your menagerie in the cloakroom, though. How many cats do you have here?'

Um. Six. And a rabbit. It's… for the school project.'

'Course it is.' Mirasol produced menus from the folds of her apron. 'You know, there's something I forgot to tell you about that mad prince.'

'Oh?'

'Mm. he always leaves payment for the things he takes. Vials of medicine, firewood, that sort of thing.' Richard was careful not look at George.

'That's interesting to know, thanks.'

'What's next?' Richard asked as they dug into a meze. He was ridiculously hungry but saved a bit of aubergine to poke through the bars of Alistaire's carry case, trying to ignore a rowdy group of men in the corner. 'I think we should get to Laketown as fast as possible. There's an overnight stagecoach available somewhere, I saw a sign on the way in.'

George forked a piece of cheese with one hand, surreptitiously rubbing some of his disguise potion onto his face with the other. 'How long did it take you to reach here from Laketown?'

'About—'

'I don't know where you're from, sir, *but that is not how one human being treats another!'*

Over in the corner, one of the rowdy men had leered up at Mirasol as she passed, casually levitating a wineglass-laden tray, and tried to grab her from behind. Mirasol promptly seized the tray and clonked him over the head with it.

'*Well,*' spat the man, staggering up from his seat, wine dripping over him, 'I won't be coming here again. Filthy creepy magic users, the lot of you.'

Mirasol hissed and grabbed the man by the collar, despite being half his size. He was either very drunk or very surprised, because he made little protest as she threw him firmly out of the door. Richard tore his gaze away and turned back to George.

'It took me a few weeks, on foot and hitch hiking.' Richard felt quest rules could be twisted somewhat now he had found the Mad Prince and had several cute animals in his care. 'But the sign said the stagecoach leaves at two. We should make it to Laketown tomorrow evening.' He paused. 'I don't have enough money for the two of us though.' He glanced at the carry case. 'And I have no idea if they take pets.'

'I can take care of that,' George said confidently. Richard decided he didn't want to know.

They booked their tickets for the coach after dinner, then retreated to the inn's little back garden to allow Alistaire to sniff around. How often should you take a rabbit for a walk? Should they risk letting the cats out?

Beatrice would know. Richard was drowsy, his sense of time wonky. It was the middle of the night and his body wanted to sleep for a week, but he couldn't settle his thoughts.

'You should wear a disguise until we reach Laketown,' George said suddenly, and Richard jumped. He thought George was dozing. 'In case anyone involved with Alistaire's father's plan recognises you.'

'Good idea.' Richard had never been enchanted before. He wondered if his new face would itch. 'Splash on some of that potion.'

Half an hour later they left the inn to board the coach. Richard, now with much straighter, lighter hair and pockmarks, was about to step onto the road when one of the men from the raucous table pushed past them. His cloak slipped from his shoulder, revealing a badge on his chest emblazoned with a lightning bolt across a trident: Queen Margaret's coat of arms.

The man looked up at Richard, who thought he had been recognised. Then he realised the man was looking over his shoulder at George, who was levitating the animal cases again.

'Disgusting,' the man spat. 'You should be ashamed!'

'Of owning pets?' Richard frowned. 'We take good care of them.'

'Of your revolting habits,' the man hissed. He smelt like wine. 'No self-respecting person should engage in such unnatural behaviour.' He made a sign with his hands, as though he were warding off evil, and stomped back to his convoy.

'Two boys travelling together is not that strange,' Richard remarked when they were installed in their coach and the animals freed from their cases. 'The Duke of Lumiere is married to a man.'

'I think he means magic.'

'Oh. I suppose it really must be unpopular in Stormhaven.'

'I suppose it must.' George looked drawn and anxious, even with a small cat climbing up his arm. 'Why do you think Alistaire was sent to kidnap you?'

'There's been rebellion in my father's kingdom for years,' Richard admitted hesitantly. He had never spoken to anyone outside the family about this. He barely liked to think of himself. 'A lot of people think my father is too close to King Emmanuel and Queen Hazel. They think he should be more like Queen Margaret; stricter and less involved with people's everyday lives.'

'I don't know much about the Kingdom of Mirrors,' George confessed. 'I enjoyed reading about Princess Amelia and the dragon, though.'

'Amelia is really nice,' Richard acknowledged. In fact, she was probably his only friend outside court. Or at all.

'Can't your father stamp out rebels? My aunt—' George paused, like he had said too much. 'Don't worry. Go on.'

Richard shook his head. 'We're a constitutional monarchy, not an absolute monarchy. My father's power lies in the High Council, and if they don't support him… There's a clause in the constitution stating that it would only require the vote of nine of the twelve members to remove him from power.'

'That's another reason you wanted to find me,' George said. 'To prove your family deserves the throne.'

Richard swallowed. 'Maybe. On some level. Yes. But. But… it would only take nine votes to oust the king and queen. Alistaire pretty much confessed that Lord Eaton's been rallying enough support on the Council to stage a coup. Why would Stormhaven lords be involved with that?'

The journey ticked by slowly, as the sun rose and filled the coach with golden light. They stopped at an inn for half an hour, and Richard couldn't help staring around at other customers, wondering if they would run into the gang of men again. He considered sending word ahead to warn his parents of their arrival but didn't want to risk the note being intercepted.

Over in the corner, a couple with two small children were curled in their seats wearing travelling clothes. Several cases sat at their feet. Richard heard one of the children ask their mother, 'Can we really do magic here?' She nodded and smiled, yawning widely. 'We won't be sent to the Skeleton Rooms?' She shook her head. Richard thought of Princess Amelia and her request for a meeting with King Richard. He had been away so long he wasn't sure if the meeting had already happened. He made a mental note to ask about the Skeleton Rooms on his return.

George once more paid for their meal, from a pouch of coins that didn't seem to get any lighter.

'Are you creating money?' Richard asked when they were back in the stagecoach.

'No.' George frowned. 'I borrowed it.'

'From another person's bag?' Richard realised his tone was accusatory a second too late. A flash of anger crossed George's face.

'Where I'm from, princes don't steal.'

'They don't where I'm from either,' Richard pushed his glasses up his nose. 'I'm sorry. I know you wouldn't… but how do I actually know for sure that you're a prince?'

George sat forward, but before he could do anything, Richard said, 'If you turn me into a rabbit, there's no way you'll get access to the palace. Besides, I told you about the issues on my father's council. It's your turn to talk.'

George scowled and threw himself back in his seat, almost squashing a kitten.

Richard rolled his eyes. 'You're like my sister when she won't admit she's escaped from school, even though we just found her hiding in the kitchens. Fine. You're one of Queen Margaret's nephews, aren't you? Tell me why you ended up in that tower.'

George looked at the floor, then clicked his fingers. The carriage doors locked themselves. Both their disguises faded as George looked everywhere except for Richard's face. 'Queen Margaret banished me to solitary confinement,' he said eventually. 'You know the Stormhaven royal family? Margaret's got six younger brothers, eight children, at least thirty nieces and nephews and about a thousand grandchildren.'

'Yes...'

'There used to be seven brothers.' He sighed. 'My father was Queen Margaret's very youngest sibling. I was his very youngest child.' Richard waited.

'I killed him.'

Well. Richard was not expecting that.

George looked faintly amused at Richard's expression. 'By accident. I created a dragon, accidentally, when I was a child. When I was learning how to do *magic*—' he spat the word— 'and didn't really understand my abilities.' He exhaled, an old man again. 'To cut a long story short, the dragon killed a lot of people, including my father. I was held responsible, because the dragon was mine.'

Richard said nothing, trying not to look as though any of this conversation was unsettling.

George was looking at the wall again. 'I was eight and I was sentenced to the worst punishment you can receive after the death penalty. Some people think that it is worse, because being in isolation can send people insane.' His voice could have cut diamonds. 'I had an armed guard to the tower, but that was to be my last contact with anyone for the rest my life. They locked me in. The dragon, by the way, was basically made of smoke. Your friend Amelia would have sorted it out in about five seconds.'

'They expected you to survive by yourself?' Richard couldn't help interrupting. '*How?*'

'Magic is completely taboo in Stormhaven. As far as they were concerned, if I could conjure a dragon, I could conjure a sandwich.'

'That makes perfect sense.' Richard huffed and leant back in his seat. 'Sorry, go on.'

George did another tiny smile. 'After a few days I worked out how to unlock the door and wandered into the village to steal food. I dressed myself to look like a local child, just in case there were still guards about, but I needn't have worried. No one recognised me. There's no reason the locals would have done, really, Margaret's got more family than she has hairs on her head. After I'd been in the tower a while, I looked around and found that the previous inhabitant kept rather useful books on sorcery.' He swallowed. 'The rest is history.'

Richard digested this. George glowered at the wall.

'How did the kingdom just not notice your disappearance? There are rules about sending children to school!'

George shrugged. 'I think they pretended it was an accident. My father was a prince, but my mother was from a village far north. She was a… a courtesan. Margaret's got such an enormous family—I have eleven legitimate older siblings from my father's two marriages… No one missed me. When the mountain started to get a reputation for being haunted, I thought someone would put two and two together, but no one really has. I think the world's forgotten I exist. I use the disguises to keep up the mystery around the tower, because I thought Margaret might get wind that I'm not really in solitary confinement. My punishment was supposed to be for life. But there's been no reason for me to leave and actually go somewhere specific… until now.'

Richard fidgeted in his seat and racked his brain for everything he had read or heard about Stormhaven in the last year, everything changing shape as he thought about George's story. Queen Margaret de Winter ruled with strict rules and little tolerance for criminals but locking her nephew in a tower on foreign soil was pushing the boundaries a bit, even for her. Besides, relations between the three kingdoms were good, better than they had been for centuries. What was Margaret playing at?

They passed the rest of the journey in silence.

Chapter Seven

Laketown seemed smaller than Richard remembered, but it greeted him like an old friend. There was the lagoon and bridge, there were the tourists lining up to spot turtles, there were the restaurants and bistros. There was the cerise pink temple built by Kingdom of Mirrors refugees, mosaiced tiles sparkling in the evening sun. Their coach alighted at the main station, so they reapplied the disguise potion and walked the rest of the way, taking in the fresh air. George stared about in wonder, asking questions about the lagoon, the animals, the people. Richard wondered how they looked to outsiders, two teenage boys and half a dozen still-levitating animals, trudging along the waterfront to the White Palace.

Once they were in sight of the gate, Richard had George remove their disguises, then marched up to the gatehouse. 'Good evening, Mr Genovese,' he smiled at the guard. He had noticed that Princess Amelia knew all her employees, and possibly all her subjects, by name. He couldn't remember when he had resolved to do the same.

'Your Majesty! You're back... sooner than we expected.'

'Quite,' Richard smiled. 'I have a friend with me. Please could you let us in?' As the wrought iron gates were heaved open, Richard noticed one of the guards sprinting up the lawn to warn the castle of their arrival.

Queen Florence met them at the palace entrance, wrapping Richard up in a hug before he could say anything. She looked thinner and her brown skin seemed pulled tighter, but her eyes sparkled as she inspected him for injuries. 'Mother, this is Prince George of Stormhaven,' Richard said hesitantly. 'George, this is my mother, Queen Florence de la Fuente.'

'How do you do?' they both said simultaneously, both wearing carefully blank faces. Richard felt as though he had just introduced a sword to a bow and arrow.

'What is this?' Florence asked, looking at the animal cases. Alistaire had made a small deposit in his cage and was looking up at them waspishly.

'A problem,' Richard said quietly. 'We need to speak to Father, now.'

'He's in with the Council,' Florence said.

'They can't see this. Tell him—tell him there's been an accident at the mill. He'll always leave Council for that.'

Florence winced, but nodded and swept down the corridor.

Getting his father out of the Great Hall was one thing. Getting him to listen to Richard was another.

'An accident at the mill—who? When?' King Richard hurried along the corridor, strides ahead of his wife. 'Have the magicians been informed? We know how important it is to get those type of injuries looked at quickly—oh, hello Richard.'

'Hello, Father. You can, er, stop panicking now. There wasn't an accident at the mill. I need to speak to you in private.'

'There wasn't—' The king exhaled, simultaneously relieved and furious. His facial features didn't quite line up with either emotion, so he mostly looked like he had a bad case of stomach cramps. 'What on earth is so important that you needed to lie to get me out of court? And to lie about, about…'

'Sorry, Dad,' Richard said gently. 'The gods are probably cursing me. But you really need to see this.' He beckoned his parents into a side room.

'Who is this?' the king asked, eyes falling on George. He frowned, ever so slightly.

'This is Prince George of Stormhaven. George…' Richard realised he did not know George's surname.

George bowed. 'George de Winter, Your Majesty.'

'George? De Winter?'

'You, er, may know him better as the Mad Prince.' George bowed again. 'Sorry about the trouble I've caused up on the Eaton estate.'

'Oh, you don't need to apologise for that…' King Richard shook George's hand amicably. 'Are you by any chance related to Queen Margaret?'

'My father was Margaret's youngest brother.'

'She's the reason you ended up in that tower, I suppose.'

'Yes, as a matter of—'

'Speaking of Queen Margaret,' Richard said quickly. 'You two need to see this.' He removed the rabbit from the cage and tugged off the little harness.

George clicked his fingers. Within a heartbeat, Alistaire Eaton was standing in front of them.

Queen Florence recovered first. 'Oh dear.'

King Richard scratched his nose. 'This is going to be a long story, isn't it? Alistaire, does your father know you've spent a significant amount of time as a small animal?'

'No, Your Majesty.'

'Richard, could you please explain how Alistaire came to spend time as a small animal?'

When Richard had finished talking, his parents were looking between him and George as though deciding what to do about an outbreak of plague. George, helpfully, had turned Alistaire back into a rabbit.

'Well,' Florence said eventually. 'I can see why you wanted us both out of court. I can't think of a single member of the Council who *wouldn't* stage a rebellion.'

King Richard was silent for at least a minute. His shrewd brown eyes scrutinised first his son, then George. George was quieter in front of the King and Queen than he had been in the stagecoach: more like the George who Richard first met. Was that really only a day ago?

'There's only one way to settle this,' the king said finally. 'Let's go to the High Council and ask them about it.'

To say the High Council looked surprised to see Richard was an understatement. The Valley High Council was organised like the Kingdom of Mirrors', with eleven elected members. Today they perched on high-backed olive wood seats sat in a crescent moon shape, looking out onto the hall. Seven seats were occupied by women of varying age and identical gold jewellery. Four were occupied by men of identical age and varying gold jewellery. At least six councillors were looking at George as though seeing a ghost.

'My son has returned from his quest!' King Richard called. His tone was bright, but he gripped his wife's hand tightly. 'He seems to have brought a friend with him! Well, two friends, actually. Lord Eaton, do you know where your son is?'

'He is at school—'

'That was a rhetorical question,' the king said cheerfully. 'Mr de Winter, could you please do the honours?'

Richard picked Alistaire out from his cage and George clicked his fingers. In a flash Alistaire was back in front of them. He looked a little seasick.

'Son, what are you doing here?' Lord Eaton demanded. 'Shouldn't you be back at—back at—' he glanced at the king.

'I was just following your orders!' Alistaire wailed.

'Preposterous! What orders? Me?'

'You are quite a bad actor,' King Richard said grimly. 'I demand you both tell me what is going on!'

'I can help with that.' George snapped his fingers and a small glass jar, full of brilliant green dust, appeared in his other hand. 'This is truth dust,' George said. 'Whoever comes into contact with it can't lie for five minutes.'

He took a pinch and threw it over Alistaire's head. Alistaire squeaked. Richard was glad, just for a moment, that the entire Council was there to see Alistaire's face as the dust settled on his hair.

'Let's test it,' Richard suggested. Before anyone had time to protest, Richard asked, 'Alistaire, what's your middle name?'

'Names, probably,' George murmured.

'Rothschild Stefanos.' Alistaire said after a moment.

'See?' George said to the councillors. 'No one makes that up.' Over in his chair, Lord Eaton rather looked as though he wished he had allowed his wife to choose different names.

Richard wanted to be extra sure the dust worked. 'Alistaire, what made you choose to wear that velvet jacket under your armour?'

'My mother always told me it brings out the green in my eyes.'

George inspected Alistaire's face. 'Well, she's not wrong.' He turned to the king. 'Your Majesty, my magic works. Let's get the truth out of him.'

'Alistaire, why did you really follow Prince Richard on this quest?' King Richard asked.

'To lock him in the tower with the Mad Prince while the High Council initiated a coup.'

Richard's insides froze. It was one thing suspecting Alistaire of treason, but quite another to hear it confirmed.

'On whose orders?'

'My father's.'

Before anyone else could react, George had crossed the room and thrown the remainder of the dust over Lord Eaton. The guards recovered their senses and barrelled toward him, tackling him and pinning his arms. Either he was very surprised to be caught or very unsurprised, because he didn't make much of an effort to escape.

King Richard wasted no time. 'State your name, my Lord.'

'Ignacio Miguel Benjamin Edwardo Christos Isaac Lucas Eaton.'

'Well, I think we can be certain you aren't lying. Lord Eaton, did you know that the so-called Mad Prince was actually a child from a neighbouring kingdom?'

'Yes.'

'Did you know he is one of Queen Margaret's nephews?'

'Yes.'

'When did you learn this?'

'As soon as he arrived. Years ago. I—I was paid for the use of the tower near my estate and told to pretend it was haunted. I think she—they—knew he would work out how to get around the locked door.'

'She?' the king wore the same expression as the time he discovered his children had turned his favourite dressing gown into a flag for a game.

'Her Majesty. The Queen. Margaret de Winter.' Richard glanced at George. His face was stony and blank, but his cheeks were flushed slightly. One hand made a fist.

'This just gets better,' King Richard said through gritted teeth. 'We'll come back to your treason and false imprisonment. As well as the fact you presumed to own an ancient tower and took rent money for it. Now, why did you send Alistaire to the tower to intercept my son?'

'Our plan was to hold him hostage.'

'Whose plan?'

'We don't have a name.'

'Who is involved, then?'

'Lord Moreau, Lady Moreau, Lord de Silva, Lord Diamandis, Lady Mayfair. The Duke of Stormhaven Town.'

King Richard lost his composure for a second. The Duke of Stormhaven Town was one of Queen Margaret's most trusted advisors; one was rarely seen without the other. All the other people Lord Eaton named were sitting in the hall. The guards not restraining Lord Eaton moved swiftly, and menacingly, to block the doors.

King Richard took a deep breath. 'Why did you decide to hold my son hostage? I notice your son is wearing Durante colours.'

'We planned to blame the Durantes to drive a wedge between the Valley and the Kingdom of Mirrors. Our aim was to drain the kingdom's resources with our ransom demands and take advantage of the instability to stage a coup and depose you.'

'I must say,' King Richard said after a moment. 'I'm surprised you all had it in you to be so organised. Deciding a budget for local schools is difficult enough.'

'And you are a weak king! You allowed immigrants to flood the Valley! You almost bankrupted the country to fight the Sapphire Dragon!' George's truth dust made way for vitriol that had clearly been lurking in the depths of Lord Eaton for some time. 'Queen Margaret should unite the Three Kingdoms—she is the rightful ruler of this land and the sooner she takes your place in this throne room, the better!'

King Richard exhaled loudly and rubbed his temples. 'Well, I'm glad you've got that off your chest, Ignacio. Guards, please take them all to the dungeon. Florence, children, let's have dinner.'

Chapter Eight

It was strange being back in the castle. It was stranger having a friend there too. At dinner, Beatrice tackled Richard with a bear hug, showed him her newly-removed tooth—'I put an iron on a piece of string and dropped it down the stairs!'—and demanded Mrs Snuffles return to her clutches. She took to George immediately, asking to see magic tricks and throwing Richard dirty looks over the table, as though he had failed in his brotherly duties by neglecting to develop magical abilities.

George, who had been given a spare room and his own butler, looked a little bemused at the extensive selection of cutlery next to each plate and seemed relieved that the first course was soup.

After hearing about his journey north, which took most of the meal, Richard's parents turned their attention to the day's events.

'This plot was about more than driving a wedge between the two nations,' Florence pointed out as she poured wine. Beatrice had fallen asleep at the table, cradling Mrs Snuffles. 'Queen Margaret knows relations between the Valley and the Kingdom are too good to be ruined by one staged kidnapping. I mean, we weren't really going to fall for the Durante family crest on Alistaire Eaton's armour, for gods' sake. I think she wants us distracted. But from what?'

'The refugee crisis.'

George had not spoken throughout the meal. Everyone blinked at him.

'Think about it. People have been fleeing into the Kingdom of Mirrors through the Valley of Dreams for months—I've seen them from my tower. There are hundreds of families heading south. Why, when the economy in Stormhaven is brilliant? There is education, healthcare, a standard of living that frankly you can't get in the Kingdom of Mirrors. Yet people have been choosing to move to the south, somewhere that up until a few months ago was infected with an actual dragon. Something is happening in Stormhaven that's driving people out.'

'I think you're right.' The king frowned. 'We've planned a meeting with the Kingdom of Mirrors—we'll bring it forward. I want to speak to the whole family, including Amelia. Can we reach the Duke of Lumiere? He lives in Stormhaven. He may have information.'

'Ask him about the Skeleton Rooms,' Richard said suddenly.

'The what?' King Richard blinked.

'The Skeleton Rooms. I heard someone mention it, one of the refugees. It doesn't sound like a funfair, does it?'

They sat in silent contemplation for a minute, until George excused himself to go to bed.

'Please make yourself at home.' Florence said, standing up to hug him gently. 'You're welcome to stay with us as long as you like.'

George looked at the floor over Florence's shoulder for a moment, before tentatively hugging her back. 'Thank you.'

After George had shut the door, Richard turned to his parents. 'You knew it was George in that tower all along, didn't you?'

Florence pulled a face. 'No. Not entirely. There have been rumours for years about the way Margaret treats her prisoners and her enemies. I remembered Prince George as a child. I enquired after him once, but it was as though he had never existed. It wasn't long after that that the Eaton villagers started reporting their haunting.'

'Why didn't you say anything? He was—he is—a child! What if it were me locked away?'

Both parents looked uncomfortable. 'We can't act based on rumour, Richard,' his father said eventually. 'If we did, we'd be declaring war every five minutes. We should have made more of an effort to find out, but running a country takes up a bit more time than you'd think.'

'Couldn't you have given me a hint for my quest, at least?'

'Richard. We both know that's not how quests work.' Queen Florence rubbed her eyes. 'I'm sorry it took this long for us to be honest with each other.'

'I'm sorry too.'

'Anyway, I'm glad you've made a friend.'

'Um. Thanks.'

'Are you sure you're just friends?' King Richard asked with a gleam in his eye.

'Dad, we literally met yesterday. Gods. I'm going to bed too.' Richard rolled his eyes and pushed back his chair. His parents grinned at each other.

Chapter Nine

In a hastily arranged trial that gripped the nation, Lord Eaton and his co-conspirators were found guilty of treason, attempted kidnap and false imprisonment of a child. The most interesting revelation at the trial was the Duke of Stormhaven Town's involvement in the plot to kidnap Richard. It rather appeared he had suggested most of it.

Lady Eaton and Alistaire had disappeared, Lady Eaton spiriting her son from the palace by claiming that he was working entirely under orders from his father and not bright enough to have come up with anything himself. Their manor stood abandoned. Villagers on the estate reported that they were seen in a carriage heading toward Stormhaven, with most of their staff following in another carriage. 'We probably won't be able to extradite them,' King Richard sighed at dinner one evening. 'But I'm more interested in holding Margaret to account for her treatment of you, sir.'

'Me?' George looked superbly uncomfortable at being addressed as 'sir'.

'Locking children in towers is illegal here,' the king pointed out. 'We checked. Again, I can't apologise for how sorry I am on behalf of the Valley—'

'It's fine,' George said, looking even less comfortable. 'Honestly.'

'I still think you should see a therapist,' Florence insisted. She had spoken of relatively little else since meeting George. 'I want to make sure you're in good health.'

'I'm not sure—'

'Pick your battles,' Richard advised. George shrugged.

'Okay, then.'

'Would you ever consider returning to Stormhaven?' Florence continued. Richard almost choked on a bit of chicken. 'It is technically your home,' she reminded George gently. 'Do you want to go back?'

'If it's all right with you,' George said quietly, 'I think I'd like to stay in Laketown for good. I'd like to go to school here.'

'That can be arranged!' Florence beamed. 'It will be nice for Richard to have someone his own age around. Someone who reads, I mean.'

'Another thing,' King Richard put in. 'Eventually people will realise who you are. I don't think we should advertise that your aunt locked you away, but I'm not sure we should hide it either. What do you think?'

George considered. 'I think… I would like a normal life for a while. If people find out…' he shrugged. 'Let's just see what happens.'

The king nodded. 'Very well. We'll leave it up to you.'

George looked at his plate. 'Thank you. For—for everything.'

'You're going to regret saying that when she makes you wear crochet jumpers,' Richard said grimly.

Finer details of Richard's quest and its connection to the failed Eaton Plot, as the press were calling it, had not been released, although it was obvious that the haunted tower was no longer in use. Officially, George was the son of a minor duke from Stormhaven, but it was probably only a matter of time before the towerian fan club put two and two together. In the meantime, Richard was looking forward to getting back to his life—and to catching up on all the homework he missed while questing.

George had joined Richard's school, which was very, very strange. He adapted to Laketown life quickly, enchanting his teachers and Madame Demetria especially. He was, it turned out, quite well-educated for someone with no record of having been educated.

'Where did you learn to fight like that?' Madame Demetria had asked when she saw him sparring in the courtyard with Richard, eyeing the dagger he wore at his belt and the easy way he gripped a long silver sword.

George shrugged. 'I used to go to classes on the Eaton estate.' Richard couldn't believe that the reclusive boy prisoner had a busier social life than he did.

Two weeks later, it was the last garden party of the year, held on a fine autumn day and with rather more hot chocolate and mulled wine than in the summer months. George was the picture of aristocratic grace. Every visitor was greeted with a smile, every name remembered, every intrusive question politely deflected.

'Ah, Prince Richard.' It was Grant Westborough, resplendent in a saffron waistcoat that looked a bit like carpet. 'It was so wonderful that you didn't die on your quest.'

'Wasn't it just?' Richard replied, smiling. He added a cream cake to his plate. 'I was quite delighted at having survived.'

'Is it true that you spoke to the Mad Prince?' Grant asked. He appeared to have washed his face in some sort of industrial oil and used the residue to style his hair. He looked rather like he had fallen into the lagoon. Richard could not decide if this was a new look for Grant, or if he had just never noticed it before.

'Yes, actually—' Richard began.

'Oh, really? And what did he say to you?' Grant leered over his glass.

'I offered him a drink and drew up a chair.'

George was at Richard's shoulder. He was impeccably dressed, his hair slicked neatly back. Possibly that was the look Grant had been going for.

Grant blinked. 'And you are?'

'George,' George said, extending a hand. 'Son of a minor duke. Here to continue my magical education. I believe you, sir, once defeated an army of dissident republicans? How admirable. Can I get you another drink? Oh, let Richard get them. He has got rather good taste, you know. Really has a knack for knowing the good stuff from the bad stuff.'

'Wait, did you say you're the Mad Prince—'

'Did I? So I did. I suppose I can't be the son of a minor duke, then.'

Richard held back a laugh at Grant's face and led George away before he could turn anyone into a domestic pet.

'My secret's out, then,' George said as they walked across the lawn.

'Looks like it.' Richard realised that this was the first time he had ever enjoyed a garden party with his peers. He glanced across at George. His hair was white in the autumn sun and something about the fresh air made him seem younger, more like a normal teenager than usual. He caught Richard's eye and whatever Richard had been about to say disappeared from his head completely. He turned away, flushed.

Lady Rathbone met them at the drinks table. Like her niece, she had taken an immediate shine to George and insisted on asking him to demonstrate a magical skill every time they met. Today she had him turn her hair from black to white, then back again. 'By the way,' she added, 'there's a story in the *Valley Chronicle* about you two.'

'Wonderful,' Richard replied. He took the newspaper she offered, George peering over his shoulder. *JUST GOOD FRIENDS?*' the headline demanded. Underneath were two hundred words on the odds of Richard abdicating to marry a foreign national.

'What do you think?' George asked after he had finished reading. His tone was casual.

'I think… I think they've got five typos in this article.'

'Six.'

'Really, where?' Richard scanned the text.

'The headline. We're not good friends. You helped me properly leave my tower and we foiled a kidnap attempt. That makes us *best* friends.'

'Oh, of course.' Richard inhaled the autumn air, the afternoon stretching out in front of them. Perhaps he could ask George to show him how truth dust worked. Perhaps they could look up the Skeleton Rooms. Perhaps they could take Bean for a walk. He grinned suddenly.

'What?' George asked. He incinerated the newspaper with a wave of his hand.

'I've just remembered, I know an opera company we can use for the wedding.'

In Richard's experience, there were two types of hero: the storybook type and the type who embarked on terrifying quests by themselves and made friends with their enemies. Richard definitely still preferred reading about both types to trying to emulate them, but as he and George crossed back across the lawn to the party it occurred to him that, if someone asked, he could probably have a go at it again. Not for a while, though. He had some reading to catch up with.

The Businessman's
Daughter

Chapter One

Discontent was brewing in the Three Kingdoms, but Esme Delacroix's life already offered relatively little contentment, so she initially failed to notice how bad things were getting. Esme lived in a low-roofed inn on the Queen's Road in Stormhaven, just after the border with the Valley of Dreams. Or just before the border, if you were heading the other way. Most people were.

Stormhaven had just begun to tiptoe into spring, and Esme was glad to see the back of a desolate wintertime. During winter months everything was either brown or grey, from the sky to the hills to the sea in the distance.

Stormhaven formed the northernmost third of the crescent moon of the Three Kingdoms. It was incredibly mountainous, held the Kingdoms' only natural hot spring and, instead of beaches, boasted mile after mile of treacherous cliffs that gave way to a petulant sea. Stormhaven's trade was almost entirely based around the hot spring, a spectacular ski resort perched on a distant, snowy mountain peak and its bountiful production of goat's cheese.

Esme's village was one of a string that lined the Queen's Road. All made up of pale stone buildings, pine trees and the odd set of shops, the Queen's Road villages existed almost entirely for people on their way to somewhere else, so no one had ever bothered naming them. The Queen's Road border crossing, although a cluster of official buildings barely a mile wide, was the main border checkpoint between Stormhaven and the rest of the Three Kingdoms. Elsewhere on the boundary was too steep, too craggy or too full of wild wolves to bother putting up more than a fence.

Esme had never left her part of the Queen's Road, not even on a day trip up to the mountains or down to the Valley of Dreams. She *had* read a lot about the Valley of Dreams and the Kingdom of Mirrors and met a great deal of natives of each kingdom, so despite recent newspaper headlines she was sure there was only one real difference between Stormhaven and the rest of the Three Kingdoms. The Kingdom of Mirrors may have bizarre architecture and an eccentric royal family, and the Valley may have magnificent universities and gorgeous vineyards—and they both had nicer beaches—but the three kingdoms of the Three Kingdoms, despite what they told themselves, were quite similar. Similar scorching summers and damp winters. Similar friendly people, similar bright cuisine. By her teens, Esme was virtually certain that the three kingdoms could well have been one kingdom.

Except for the thing nobody spoke about.

For most of Esme's fourteen years, Carmel's Inn (which Esme's father, Thomas, had named after her mother in a fit of sentimentality a couple of decades before) was a busy, friendly rest stop for every sort of traveller on the Queen's Road. In the six months following the Eaton Plot, however, tourism to Stormhaven had almost entirely dried up. The Queen's Road was normally crowded during winter with tourists heading north to sample the hot spring, but this year visitors were as rare as visits from the Queen herself.

As a result, the inn's twelve rooms were no longer full to the rafters and Esme was no longer roped in to help behind the bar and/or at the reception desk and/or in the laundry room before and/or after school. The inn had taken only half of its usual winter turnover; her parents were thinking of letting their two full-time employees go.

Esme did not think it fair that the three monarchies' political bickering was ruining her family's livelihood. King Richard and Queen Florence, stung by the kidnap attempt on their son, exasperated by Queen Margaret's audacity to imprison her nephew on their land and fully suspicious of everyone Lord Eaton may or may not have ever met, had imposed strict trade embargoes on Stormhaven. They also released multiple statements recommending his citizens holiday elsewhere. King Emmanuel and Queen Hazel, whose own kingdom was faring much better now it no longer suffered from a dragon infestation, followed suit.

These trade restrictions resulted firstly in Stormhaven facing an olive oil shortage, secondly in it facing a wine shortage and thirdly in Queen Margaret retaliating by strengthening her side of the border with more armed guards (which was odd, given that her government denied any involvement with the Eaton Plot and frequently published statements expressing deep sadness at such false accusations). What was once a friendly checkpoint with perfunctory paperwork was now staffed by fifty officials and heavily patrolled by the sort of men who could lift trees over one shoulder but not count past one hundred. These changes did nothing to encourage tourism or inter-kingdom trade and contributed to a steadily shrinking economy.

Making winter colder still were the whispers, carried along the Queen's Road like the plague, that people were starting to vanish at rates too high to ignore. Even the steadfastly law abiding knew of a healer arrested at the bed of a sick child, or of a discreet circle of scholars apprehended as they pored over ancient textbooks. Few in Stormhaven would admit if someone magical lurked within their family tree, but many looked into their depleted store cupboards and concluded that although the south might be full of occultists and tricksters, it was preferable to living under Queen Margaret's increasingly totalitarian thumb.

Over the winter the exodus had grown to an extent that Esme could watch the lines for the border from her bedroom window, despite the inn being about a mile from the checkpoint. Travellers faced queues of days or even weeks, laden with belongings and huddled in tents as they waited their turn. Merchants and those wealthy enough to pay a bribe could skip to the front, but even they faced queues behind other merchants doing exactly the same thing.

Now the weather was warming up, Esme knew her parents were hoping to see an influx of customers from both sides of the border, stopping off on their way to visit friends and family in other kingdoms, or conducting what little trade they could. In the meantime, the family business had diversified. Carmel had taken to bringing the inn's comforts out to the border queues. She would get up before dawn each day, pack a small cart with coffee, honeyed pastries and hot rolls, and sell them to the hundreds of people huddled on the roadside. Thomas had turned part of the parlour into a study for travellers to get their papers in order.

Esme's fortunes began to take a particularly depressing turn on a Saturday not long after her fourteenth birthday. After her homework, Esme spent the morning organising the inn's storage room, down in the basement. Stocks of goat's milk soap, sugared almonds and kumquat liqueur, bought from local friends and sold on to tourists, lived on one side, organised by price and Carmel's incredibly detailed labelling system. Olives, olive oil, wine and olive soap imported from the south before the embargo lived on the other, organised by weight (and Carmel's incredibly detailed labelling system). Why the kingdoms bothered trading soaps in the first place, Esme had no idea. Sorting it all kept her busy, at least. Well. Slightly busy. Busy until lunchtime.

Ironically, the most precious stock of all sat in a hidey hole under the floorboards, wrapped in old newspaper and rags Esme had discarded from her sewing box, to be traded under the cover of darkness while her father visited his aunt two villages along.

'How are you, Miss Esme?' asked a guest as Esme emerged from the basement. 'How have your fits been since I was last here?'

'Oh, Madame Velazquez, I didn't know you were back on the Queen's Road!' Esme greeted one of the inn's regulars with a smile. 'They're just fine at the moment, thank you. How was your journey?'

'Epilepsy, isn't it?' Madame Velazquez had been travelling the Three Kingdoms as long as Esme could remember. The last time she passed through the inn, she was heading to the War Relief Festival at Scavenger's Ruin with a suitcase full of bathing suits.

'Yes, epilepsy.'

'And you're getting treatment for it?'

'Of course, Madame Velazquez, I see a specialist in Stormhaven Town every six months,' Esme lied. She left her guest at the stairs and continued to the reception.

Esme loathed weekends. On school days, she could flit from the classroom to the inn to a shop with her friends without having time to pause. At the weekend, Esme had time to herself, and whenever her mind was idle, she was likely to suffer a fit. Her friends would have envied any moment of peace and quiet. 'I would love to have ten minutes to read a book,' her friend Georgiana would say wistfully. 'Instead I have three siblings to look after while Mum's at the port and Dad's on border patrol.'

That was one upside to all the diplomatic disputing: Queen Margaret had invested in so much border security, on land and at Stormhaven's three ports, that anyone who lived nearby could find employment. On the downside, the pay was awful. Georgiana's mother lived away from home for three weeks at a time, patrolling the harbour. Every boat, whether a tiny fishing skiff or enormous cargo ship, was searched upon arrival and before it left the port. Little patrol dinghies rowed along the coast, upsetting local mermaids so much that they were threatening to unleash their pet sharks into Stormhaven waters. Of course, mermaids were officially banned from Stormhaven waters, so the patrol responded by shooting at them with poisoned arrows.

Reaching the reception, Esme almost tripped over the luggage of a new set of guests. A large man in his fifties loomed over the foyer, surrounded by enough cases and bags for a circus. Judging by his rich brown skin, he was from the Kingdom of Mirrors, but he was dressed in the sort of finery you only got from enjoying years as a wealthy merchant, so he probably hadn't lived there for a while. His wife, a much younger olive-skinned woman with a tiny waist and glossy hair, stood reading a newspaper as she waited for their bags to be brought in. The headline bellowed, '*GOVERNMENT OPERATION UNCOVERS DEADLY MAGIC CULT!*' A daughter, around Esme's age, stood to one side.

'Can I take your bags?' Esme tucked her curls behind her ears, straightened her dress and hurried toward them, noticing that up close the wife was as old as her husband.

'Of course,' she snapped, her eyes on her paper. The subheading hissed, '*Ten so-called magicians found in possession of spell books and prayer shrines are taken into questioning on suspicion of enchantment of everyday objects.*' 'Don't just stand there.'

'Which room are you in?'

'If you work here, you should know.'

Over at the reception desk, her father mouthed, 'Three and four,' then rolled his eyes at her. Esme grinned and grabbed the first case. The name *Alexandre Beauchamp* was embroidered on the side.

'Violet,' called the wife, glancing over at her daughter, 'you're supposed to be keeping out of our way this trip.'

The daughter looked up. She was probably the person her mother had in mind when instructing her magician to make her look younger, but her high cheekbones, creamy walnut skin and smooth, chocolatey hair suited her. On her mother they looked, well, like someone who had instructed their magician to make them look twenty-five years younger.

'Is that a sketchpad by your bag?' Esme asked. 'There's an art studio a couple of villages along. It's only small but I can show you it if you'd like?'

'No thank you,' Violet replied. 'I can find it myself.'

How polite.

That evening, the Beauchamp family were in the restaurant when Esme had a fit.

Fit was not quite the right word for what Esme experienced but, along with words like *epilepsy* and *episode*, it was the closest way she could think of explaining her unwanted extra skill in public without arousing suspicion. Really it was this: Esme going about her life in a corner of the restaurant, stacking a tray full of used plates and wondering if she would have time that evening to go through a new sewing pattern she had bought from the village. The dress was complicated, but not too—

Esme's eyes rolled back into her head, her insides were being squeezed outside and then she could *see*:

Bertie the kitchen hand, striding past with a tureen of hot soup. A small child running across the restaurant at full pelt, paying no attention to the man with his hands full of a dish of steaming liquid, Bertie tripping and the tureen flying from his grasp—

Esme opened her eyes. Bertie the kitchen hand was striding past with a tureen of hot soup.

'Careful!'

Esme scooped up the child, pulling him from Bertie's path by a hair's breadth. They were so close Esme could feel steam on her face. Bertie wobbled a little but stayed upright. 'Not bad, Esmeralda. I didn't know you'd had an episode.'

Esme was breathing hard, nauseous. 'I didn't—this one was really quick. I just saw—' she glanced around to check if any of the guests were listening, but no one seemed to have noticed how narrowly Esme avoided a horrific accident. 'I *just* saw it happen. This one was quicker than normal. I mean—the boy was right there—it happened instantly—' she was so out of puff that she didn't even correct Bertie for using her full name.

As Esme cleared the last of the tables later that evening, the girl from reception wandered over, tapping a pencil against her palm. Her parents were arguing with Bertie over the bill.

'Hi… Violet. Can I get you anything?' There was a pause, for so long Esme thought Violet had misheard her.

'Can I—'

'Esme isn't usually a diminutive of Esmeralda, is it?'

Esme froze.

'No. No it isn't, but I never liked being called Esmeralda, so I asked my parents to call me Esme.'

'I prefer Esmeralda. It means emerald, doesn't it? Like your eyes.'

Esme couldn't breathe. Lights danced at the edge of her vision.

'I just wanted to say, that was a really good save earlier. I don't think his mother noticed anything was about to happen.'

By the time Esme's vision cleared, Violet was gone.

Chapter Two

Esme spent the next week helping her parents with the inn, trying not to think about Violet Beauchamp and failing miserably. Even the spectacular collection of illegal goods in the basement couldn't distract her.

Although every ingredient was by itself innocuous, many of them, when put together and traded by Esme's parents without the knowledge of Her Majesty's Revenue and Customs, gave off a distinct whiff of magical activity. Boxes of herbs, tiny glass vials, heavy iron cauldrons and sets of crystal balls would all give rather the wrong impression to the government. The most important stock of all, however, was the books. Fat spell books, tiny pocket manuals of household charms, instruction manuals on reading the tarot, histories of the witches of the Kingdom of Mirrors. Possession of just a few pages would get you six months in the Stormhaven Town prison, or worse… Esme did not like to think what a small library could do to her parents.

Early one morning, Esme accompanied Carmel down to the queue of travellers at the border. They charged very little for the food they sold, and Carmel was not averse to giving it away for free to those who looked the most exhausted. A cold snap overnight left a chill in the air and travellers were burning newspapers for warmth. Esme watched a headline go up in flames: *'PRINCE RICHARD AND PRINCE GEORGE ATTEND UNIVERSITY OPENING WITH QUEEN FLORENCE: 10 SIGNS WE CAN EXPECT A ROYAL BETROVAL IN THE SPRING.'* Next to it, another newspaper crackled into ash: *'WHY WE SHOULD STOP TRYING TO MARRY YOUNG ROYALS OFF TO ONE ANOTHER BEFORE THEY REACH ADULTHOOD.'*

'Where have you travelled from?' Carmel asked one young woman who was nursing a baby on a small dirty rug. 'That cloak seems rather heavy, even for this time of year. Are you not hot?'

'We've come from Star's Point,' the woman replied. Star's Point was the last village at the tip of the crescent moon. It was cold enough to snow some of the year. Very few people lived there.

'You've travelled hundreds of miles,' Carmel said in surprise. 'Just you and the baby?'

The woman nodded. 'My husband was taken six weeks ago. That's when I knew we had to leave.'

'Taken? By whom?' Carmel's maternal instincts could not be quelled. She poured the woman an extra cup of orange juice and handed her a hot roll.

'By...' The woman looked around, fearful. 'By them.'

Carmel leant forward. Esme, against her better judgement, did too. 'He was taken to the prison?' Carmel asked.

'I think so.' The lady sniffed and her baby started to grizzle. 'That's what the guard said when they came for him.'

'What had he done?' Esme asked.

'Esme, you can't—'

'He was working on a potion to cure measles. He had found a book in an old house and was trying to replicate the recipe. One of the neighbours must have seen...' She blinked back tears. 'I knew someone who worked near the Skeleton Rooms. They said that... they said...' either she could not or would not say any more. The baby wailed.

'When you're in the Valley, go down to the royal palace in Laketown,' Carmel urged. 'The court should hear about what happened to your husband. They've been having meetings with Lumiere every five minutes since the Eaton Plot, you would think they could spend a moment hearing about what it's like living up here.'

'What can they do?' Esme asked when they were walking home. 'The monarchy at Laketown, I mean. At Lumiere. What can they realistically do for ma—for people with—for people like me? We don't even know if the Skeleton Rooms are real or not, we've just heard people whispering about them. It. Surely we would all notice if a prison popped up somewhere?'

Carmel readjusted her hold on the food cart. 'It's real. Real as the bloody queen. Real as the thing we have to pretend is epilepsy. Real as the shrines they keep confiscating off people who just want something to believe in.' She took a deep breath. 'Come on, we've got to help your father with breakfast.'

They passed the Beauchamp family coming down to the restaurant as they entered the inn. Esme looked at the floor until she knew they were out of view.

A couple of days later, Esme calculated that she was spending approximately three hours per day trying not to think about Violet Beauchamp and at least forty minutes per day actively thinking about Violet Beau-champ, which equalled too many minutes of dedication to a human with whom she had exchanged less than thirty seconds' conversation. Esme told herself that she was preoccupied with Violet because she was an unusual guest.

Most of the time, a guest was just a guest. Esme disliked some, was fond of others, and acquainted with a few regulars. But no matter how pleased they were with her order taking, nor how charmed by her endless smile, freckled olive complexion and excellent conversational skills, Esme would always be someone they paid to bring them things. Until she met Violet, Esme hadn't considered that a guest might notice her magic and not tell anyone about it. After all, if Violet had reported Esme, she would already be in Stormhaven Town awaiting trial. Violet's sensitivity, she assured herself, was why she was preoccupied with her.

What's more, Violet was nothing like the subset of wealthy, entitled visitors the inn's staff loved to hate. She did not call for hot chocolate at three o'clock in the morning. She did not provide special instructions regarding the care of her laundry. Her breakfast did not need to be served in her bedroom. Her parents, of course, requested all these things, and more: a certain type of bath salt, specific eggs, wine at the crack of dawn. Esme was sure Violet's novelty made her, well, novel.

Eventually Esme admitted that she was lying to herself with remark-able abandon. Was it that Violet was the first guest Esme had offered to accompany to the art shop? Probably. Was it Violet's glossy mane of chestnut hair, of which Esme was simultaneously jealous and in awe of? Probably!

Esme was about to decide it was all about the hair when an episode of an entirely different type occurred.

It was dinnertime and Carmel was busy in the kitchen while Thomas took orders in the restaurant. Esme and Katerina, their other full-time employee, worked behind the bar. Violet's family stood against the bar, enjoying what had recently become quite an expensive bottle of Val-ley-produced red wine before proceeding to their table to find fault with the food.

'What do you think about this talk of a war?' Mr Beauchamp asked. He reminded Esme of the octopuses the fishing boats brought in. His puffy face suggested he was rather used to spending a lot on wine.

'Oh, Alexandre, don't ruin the evening with politics,' his wife implored. She had hardly touched her wine, even though one glass was almost as expensive as the meal they were about to eat. 'Besides, it won't come to that. King Richard and Queen Florence won't allow a war with Margaret. They know who would win.'

As with most political discussions these days, complete strangers felt the need to interrupt one another's conversations to impart special wisdom. Today it was the family in room twelve, a ferrety gentleman and a wife who never seemed able to get a word in edgeways.

'The King and Queen won't be around forever,' the ferrety man announced. 'Their son is much braver. He and that Prince George would make a good team,' he added. 'When they both come of age, I imagine they will be a formidable force in the Three Kingdoms.'

'Good team is one phrase for it,' grunted Mr Beauchamp. 'Horrendously inappropriate if you ask me.'

'Because they're from rival nations?' Violet asked. Esme could hardly hear her. Sheets of hair obscured most of her face.

'Because two men shouldn't… shouldn't…'

'Be friends?' Violet asked innocently. Esme hid a smile and tried to focus on the glasses she was drying. Ferrety man snickered audibly.

'*Carry on* together,' Mr Beauchamp said. His tone was delicate but his gaze, toward the ferrety gentleman, was vehement. 'It's not natural.'

'The Duke of Lumiere married a man,' Violet pointed out.

'Southerners roast cats on spits, you stupid girl, and need incantations to get them out of bed. The whole of the Kingdom of Mirrors is depraved. You should be grateful your mother and I never make you go down there to see the degenerates for yourself.'

'They just do things differently. Half of that stuff is just nonsense in the newspapers because no one's allowed to talk about the Skeleton Rooms and anyway, you're from Lumi—'

Esme heard a crash.

She turned to see Violet wearing her father's wine, including the glass. Esme's first thought was of injury: the glass had smashed over her head. Violet just stood there, swaying slightly. Mrs Beauchamp leaned on the bar, motionless. Ferrety man and his wife looked astounded.

'Look what you made me do.' Mr Beauchamp looked profoundly disappointed. 'Go and clean yourself up.' Violet fled. 'Waitress! Bring me more wine.'

'Of course, sir, right away.' Esme nodded to Katerina, who was watching the scene in disbelief. Katerina blinked and reached for another glass.

Esme hurried up to room four. The door was open, its Do Not Disturb sign askew. She knocked, then poked her head around the door. She could hear a tap running in the bathroom, so she ventured in slowly.

Normally, Esme loved seeing the inn's rooms in use. She was so used to seeing them empty, when they had cleaned up after their guests, that she felt a little thrill seeing them occupied. Some guests used the table to store cases, others used the cupboard. Some would work their way through the complimentary soaps and sugared almonds, others discarded them. Each time she peeked into a room in use, Esme felt like she was seeing a snapshot of their guests' lives.

Violet was looking in the bathroom mirror, pulling shards of glass from her hair. Blood dribbled from her hairline to her eyebrow. 'Are you all right?' Esme asked, then immediately berated herself. Violet's fingers were shuddering so badly she had trouble gripping the glass fragments. Her soft grey dress was badly stained and torn a little. Grazes stood out on her neck and forehead—she was lucky not to have cut her eyes. 'I can help you clean that up,' Esme offered. 'There's a first aid kit under the sink.' She made to get it, but Violet stopped her.

'I'm fine, honestly, it's just a few scratches.'

'There is blood coming out of your head.' Esme tried not to think about the fact that up close, Violet smelt a little bit like violets. 'And I can see all the cuts better than you can, I'll be quicker.'

Violet shrugged. 'All right, then.'

'Are outbursts of violence a normal thing in your family?' Esme asked as she dabbed at the cuts.

Violet shrugged again. 'Sometimes.' She was shaking underneath the cloth. Esme couldn't tell if Violet was cold or traumatised or terrified. She didn't know how to ask if *sometimes* meant *only when I upset him* or *only when he's angry about something* or *all the time, actually.*

Esme tried to remember what her teachers had taught her about dealing with abuse victims; a lesson added to the school curriculum after an incident involving one of the younger students and a trafficking gang. 'Is there anyone you could talk to about it? Would you like me to find someone you could talk to?'

'No! No, honestly, I'm fine. Please don't make a fuss, it'll only be—'

It'll only be worse if you do.

'Okay, well... I'm here if you ever want to talk to me. Any time you like. My bedroom's the one at the end of the top floor corridor.' Esme leant back to check she had disinfected every cut. The blood was already clotting and a bruise already forming, which made it look even worse. Violet's eyes were far away, gazing at something over Esme's shoulder.

When she had tidied up the first aid kit, Esme retreated to the bedroom. She looked at the desk and the barely made bed, then realised what she was seeing.

'Is that a tarot set?'

Violet followed her out of the bathroom. 'No?'

'Is that a spell book?'

'No...'

'Is that a potions kit?'

'No.'

'Violet, my eyeballs work perfectly.'

'Fine.' Violet stood over the stack of materials Esme had noticed. Although she was still shaking slightly, she looked defiant. 'Yes, these are all highly illicit magical objects. What are you going to do about them?'

'Why would I do anything about them?'

For at least five seconds, all Esme could hear was the hum of noise from downstairs. She took in the scene in front of her: well-thumbed spell books and tarot cards, pins poked into a cloth doll, half empty vials shining with viscous substances. A tin of pencils that Esme recognised from the local art shop.

'Why are you being so nice to me? Is this because of the thing with the soup the other day?' Violet sounded suspicious, or angry, or both.

'Believe it or not, some of us just want to help when we see someone in distress.' Esme headed toward to the door, abruptly tired. 'Look, you kept my secret, so I will keep yours. Both of them.'

'Wait!' Violet hurried after her, out to the landing. 'I'm—I'm sorry, I was rude. And thank you for coming to help me. Most people just turn a blind eye when he's like that in public. I'm not—I'm not used to anyone looking out for me.' Violet's eyes were slightly unfocused again.

'I shouldn't have lost my temper.' Esme paused. 'Do you want me to see if I can fix your dress?'

'You know someone who fixes dresses?'

'Yes, me.'

'Oh. Um, yes, please.' Violet ducked into her room and appeared a minute later wearing a dressing gown and holding the flimsy material. 'See you at breakfast?'

'I'll be the one clearing plates.'

Esme and Violet were friends after that, sort of. Violet seemed to avoid her parents except for mealtimes and began keeping Esme company when she did chores around the inn. Esme thought it might be awkward, the first morning Violet sought her out and soundlessly joined in with the laundry. Over the course of an hour they barely exchanged three words, but Esme found the silence comfortable, like curling up with a book on a rainy day.

Esme wondered what Violet did with herself when Esme was at school and wanted to ask more about the wineglass incident, but didn't know how to approach the subject. She found herself looking forward to going home and finishing her homework so she could get on with folding sheets or wiping down tables. Until Violet arrived, Esme hadn't minded being the only teenager working at the inn; now she wondered what she had done without Violet's quiet, steady presence. She hadn't thought her life had been lacking, before. It hadn't been. Esme's parents, gently amused by their daughter's new friendship, didn't mind Violet helping out, either, because they had a rush of guests and needed an extra pair of hands.

Mr and Mrs Beauchamp showed no signs of leaving the inn, although Esme had assumed they had stopped there on their way to or from business. Instead Mrs Beauchamp booked another week and demanded they source her thicker towels.

After a few days, Esme realised Mr Beauchamp was holding meetings in the parlour with his wife and some of the new guests: a couple of knights, a simpering woman with a Valley accent and her irritable-looking son, plus a handful of women who looked a little too like Queen Margaret for comfort. Whatever business they were doing, they did not want to be disturbed: Madame Velazquez almost got into a fight with Mrs Beauchamp over her proximity to their table.

'What does your father trade?' Esme asked Violet one afternoon as she swept the corridors.

Violet flicked a duster along a wall absently, a pencil tucked behind her ear. The cuts on her face were beginning to heal, the ugly bruise turning green. 'He's not a merchant, he works for the government. Something in security.'

'Is it a good job?' Esme was surprised someone on government pay could afford to live like the Beauchamps.

Violet shrugged. 'I think so. He works up north a lot, up at—' she stopped. 'He's just here checking up on the border crossing.'

'Checking up' was one way of putting it. Bertie cornered Esme and Carmel one evening as they cleaned the restaurant, hanging a 'DO NOT DISTURB: TOXIC CLEANING PRODUCTS IN USE' sign on the door before locking it carefully.

'I've seen him down in the basement,' Bertie hissed. 'Mr Beauchamp. And he's been sniffing around the border queue. I don't think he's just some government pen-pusher, I think he's here patrolling for magic users who are trying to leave. Or those who live here,' he added pointedly.

Carmel, who was organising tablecloths for the next day, scowled.

'We haven't given him any reason to suspect us of anything.' Esme argued. 'The basement is locked all the time. I even lock myself in when I'm in there. Anyway, Violet says he's just a government worker.'

'Violet doesn't look like someone who's included in her parents' lives,' Carmel pointed out. Esme wondered if Mr Beauchamp knew about his daughter's magic stash. 'We should charm the door so only Thomas or I can open it,' Carmel continued. 'Maybe the witch in the woods could help?'

'Do you really want to be seen going there?' Esme asked. The old lady who resided somewhere in the forest on the edge of their village was a local legend, elusive at best and evasive at worst. Word on the street was that the only reason she hadn't been arrested for openly practising magic was that she had charmed her cottage to be invisible to anyone with any sort of authority.

'Hm. Esme, I want you to be careful. Don't give him any reason to think you have the second sight.'

'Except for that one episode, I haven't done a single bit of magic since he's been here!'

Of course, the next day she had an episode.

One moment she was cleaning the kitchen during dinner service. The next:

'Esme, are you—'

Hundreds of people shuffled through mud, walking toward a huge, ancient, blackened stone castle. Guards shouted in the distance. The castle's crumbling chimneys were emitting filthy smoke; Esme realised she could taste ash. She looked around. Behind her, the line stretched for miles.

Children

Screaming

The Queen

The castle

Smoke

'Esme!'

Esme sat up. Her brain did not remember falling, but her bottom did. A plate lay in pieces. Bertie was kneeling beside her. 'You all right?' He asked urgently. 'Was it another… fit?'

'Yep.' Esme found her voice. She sat up and took several deep breaths, forcing herself to concentrate on the smell of lamb roasting, the cold bite of the stone floor and the sounds of the kitchen clanging around her.

Where had she just been? She stood up shakily and leant on the counter. 'I think I just saw the Skeleton Rooms.' She thought back to the terrified young woman with the baby. 'It's awful, it's not just some prison—'

'Sit down.' Bertie plonked her onto a storage box and handed her a steaming mug of sweet tea. Esme closed her eyes until her nausea abated, listening to her mother rush around the stove with such intent she hadn't noticed Esme fall. Was the castle in her vision where her parents would end up if anyone found out about their side business?

She opened her eyes. Bertie was still standing over her, a hulking bodyguard in a stained apron. 'I need advice.'

Bertie made toward her mother. 'Carmel!'

Esme held out a hand to stop him. 'No, magical advice. From someone who knows what they're doing. I need—I need to see the witch.'

Chapter Three

Esme rose and left the inn before dawn the next day. It took until the sun was properly overhead to reach the part of the woods where the witch supposedly lived. This was partially because the woodland was on the side of a mountain, pine trees packed so densely together that Esme could barely see the ground for pine needles. It was mostly because the directions her mother provided were terrible.

After following any path she could find, Esme stumbled out onto a tiny clearing in which a small stone bungalow sat with its chimney puffing cheerfully. On the doorstep stood a white-haired figure wearing what looked distinctly like spotted cotton pyjamas.

'You're late,' she said. 'The kettle's going to need putting on again.'

The witch looked like someone had taken an elderly lady, roasted her in an oven and showered her with potpourri. Her skin was so wrinkly it was hard to tell where her cheeks ended and her eyes began. At least four warts adorned her chin. Her hands were clawed and bony with arthritis. Her nails, though, were neatly trimmed and painted with pink varnish. Her wispy white hair, which reached her waist despite only covering half of her scalp, was plaited and decorated with flowers. She smelt, not like the decrepit visitors to the inn whose weekly wash did not quite reach every corner, but like talcum powder and rose petals. This was not a crazy old lady, Esme realised, but an elderly woman in full control of her faculties. It was conceivable the pyjamas were a conscious fashion choice.

'Were you expecting me?' A brown dog greeted Esme in the doorway, its scrubby tail wagging.

'Of course I was expecting you, dear,' the old lady replied. A gold tooth winked from the back of her mouth. 'I keep an eye on all the magical ones.'

'Great,' Esme replied. 'What have your tarot cards told you?'

'That all these secrets of yours will kill you one day,' she said amicably. 'Also, that you enjoy green tea. Here, have a cup.'

She waved her hand and there was a copper kettle and two china cups.

'Hot but not boiling water?' Esme asked, looking at the kettle.

'Of course. I'm not a heathen.'

They sat at the little table, sunshine spilling through the windows. If Esme pretended very hard, she could almost be back in her grandparents' kitchen, having tea on a Sunday afternoon. Their little house had been sold after they died of a fever, around the same time Esme started having episodes. She was probably no more than six at the time. She wondered what her grandparents would have thought of her now.

'Now, that problem of yours.' The witch interrupted Esme's attempts to rationalise the situation with a clatter of teacups.

'How did you—never mind.' Esme sipped her tea. It was perfectly brewed. 'I know something awful is happening to all the magic users. I saw—I don't know what I saw. Something bad. But how do I help? Who do I tell? How do I prove it?'

'I think you know the answers to two of those questions,' the witch replied. She munched on a biscuit.

'Princess Amelia…' Esme said. 'King Richard and Queen Florence. They would know what to do.'

'They're convening in Laketown this week,' the witch said confidently. 'They meet up about once a month.'

'To discuss the Eaton Plot?'

'To discuss the thing you saw in your vision. You don't think it's obvious that people are leaving Stormhaven? They know something's going on up here.'

'I should go to the White Palace in the Valley of Dreams and tell the court what I saw, it could help them decide what to do.' Esme sat up. 'You're right, I knew that all along. But how do I show them my vision? It might not have even happened yet. I can't record what's in my head, can I?'

'Have you not heard of literature, girl, or art? They are perfectly acceptable means of sharing what goes on in one's mind. But to communicate your vision efficiently, I fear you will need some magical help.'

'Of course I will.' Esme resisted the urge to roll her eyes. 'Go on then, what have you got? And how much will I have to pay for it?'

The witch stood and strode to a cabinet. Or shuffled with purpose, anyway. After a moment rummaging in a drawer, she produced a small glass bauble, the size and shape of a walnut.

'With some carefully worded trickery, we should be able to extract your thoughts and store them in this. When you're ready to see them, you tap it.'

'I extract my thoughts into a walnut.'

'I do it all the time.' The witch sounded affronted. 'How else would I keep track of my shopping list?'

'Okay. How do I pay you?'

'Oh, you will. One day.' The witch's tone was friendly, but Esme felt a pang of dread.

'Right. Okay. Show me how to perform this spell. Wait. I never asked you your name.' Esme felt suddenly rude, and embarrassed.

'My name?' the witch grinned. 'Esmeralda.'

Esme was so distracted upon her return from the forest that it took her a minute to realise that Violet's family was checking out. She hadn't seen Violet since the previous evening, when she briefly confided her vision of the castle whilst Violet collected her parents' wine from the bar. Violet hadn't said much, although it was hard to tell if that was because she knew something about the Skeleton Rooms and didn't want to say, or because she didn't talk much. Now her father was yelling at the reception desk and her mother was yelling at the carriage driver. Mr Beauchamp had a scratch on his cheek that looked intriguingly similar in position to one of the pins in Violet's little doll. Violet herself was nowhere to be seen. Esme took clean bed linen upstairs to their rooms, hoping she would see Violet again to return her fixed dress. She was so wrapped up in her thoughts that she didn't notice anyone until—

'Esme!'

Someone grabbed Esme's arm with force and pulled her into room four.

'Ow. What are you doing? Your parents are checking out downstairs, they're about to leave—'

Violet was busy locking the door behind them. 'They're going on business to Margaret's castle in Stormhaven Town. Before they head up to—'

'To the Skeleton Rooms? Your dad works there, doesn't he?' The suspicion had been growing in Esme's stomach since Bertie mentioned seeing Mr Beauchamp near the basement. *He works in security.*

Violet held Esme's gaze. 'Yes.' She took a deep breath. 'How was the witch in the woods? Have you decided to go to Laketown yet?'

Esme was thrown by the change of subject. 'How did you know I went to see the witch?'

'I was awake early this morning… and my eyeballs work perfectly. So, you're going to Laketown to tell them about your vision?'

'Um. Yes. How did you… never mind.'

'Look,' Violet said quickly, 'I have something to show you, before they notice I'm not with them.' She dug around behind her bed, producing a large roll of parchment. 'Is this the place you saw in your vision?'

She spread the parchment over the wooden floor. One half was a large and intricate floor plan of a sprawling castle, with five floors and at least two layers of basements. The other half was a front elevation of the castle, looking somehow menacing even as a two-dimensional architect's drawing.

'Yes.'

Violet swallowed. 'I thought so. This is the Skeleton Rooms.' Well, 'rooms' was definitely a misnomer. Esme studied the plan. Some areas were labelled 'kitchen' and 'staff quarters'. Some were labelled 'interrogation room' and 'prison cells'. Some were blacked out completely.

'How did you get these?'

'These aren't the original plans. I copied them and returned them to my father's belongings.'

'That is scarily detailed.' Esme looked at the parchment with new appreciation.

'I have something else,' Violet said after a moment. She fished behind her bed again, this time returning with a small, leatherbound notebook. She handed it to Esme, who flicked through a couple of pages.

Star's Point—S.R.—castle?

Harvest festival party—A.B. and D.S.T. meeting upstairs.

Veiled threat of Skeleton Rooms on discovery of spell book. Prison?

There were dozens of well-thumbed pages, all dated. They went back years.

'You've been keeping a diary,' Esme realised. 'Of your father's work?'

Violet nodded. 'I wanted to—to keep a record. My father used to make hints about the Skeleton Rooms to scare me. I thought he was exaggerating so I would stop doing magic, but then he started having these meetings, and he got promoted, and he would start bragging about things at home—' Her face was flushed. 'I've got names and dates. And illustrations of people he meets. I think a lot of it's classified. He, um, talks when he drinks, then threatens my mother not to say anything the next day.' Violet took a deep breath.

'When you go to Laketown, I want to come with you,' Violet indicated the notebook and parchment. 'I want to show the court these. What you saw has something to do with what my father's been up to, I know it.'

Esme thought about it. She briefly considered reasons why travelling together might not be a good idea (they barely knew each other; two unaccompanied teenagers might draw attention, which was why she had planned on asking her mother to accompany her; Mr Beauchamp looked like the sort of man who could send a small army to drag Violet back to Stormhaven). None held up under examination. 'All right. But only if you're sure.'

'I am.' Violet took another breath. Esme looked at Violet's hair, wondering what it felt like to touch. *Normal hair, obviously, honestly—*

'Then I want to stay in Laketown. I know how he treats me isn't acceptable, but he's too powerful in Stormhaven for me to do anything about it. Going down to the Valley with you while they're heading north could be my only opportunity to get away from them both. Please.'

Esme took in the mess of Violet's face. She wondered if Violet covered the bruises with make up when she went out. She imagined a much younger Violet, clutching a tin of pencils and her notebook. She thought about how Violet smelt a little bit like violets.

'Violet, you don't need to ask my permission to escape from your abusive family. To be honest, if you hadn't suggested not going with them when they left, my parents would have done. They wanted to report your dad for throwing that glass over you.'

'Really?'

'Really you don't need permission, or really my parents are furious on your behalf?'

Violet shrugged. 'Really, we should get going as soon as possible.'

Esme rolled her eyes and gathered up the parchment, trying to ignore the flutter of nervous anticipation in her stomach. 'Right, stay here and lock the door behind me. I'm going to speak to my parents.'

Ten minutes later, Violet's parents had checked out (perhaps they thought their daughter was amongst one of Mrs Beauchamp's customised shoe boxes) and Esme had cornered her parents in the laundry room.

'The vision I had last night. I saw something about the prison. I want to go to Laketown to tell the court, today. Violet wants to come with me. She can help. Then I think we should move to the Valley of Dreams or the Kingdom of Mirrors.'

She waited for her parents to argue.

Thomas rubbed his scrubby beard. 'We wondered when you were going to tell us you wanted to leave.'

'We thought we might have to tell you first,' Carmel said quietly.

'What?' Esme wasn't sure what she had been expecting her parents to say, but that wasn't it. 'Why have you never mentioned moving away?'

'This is our home and our livelihood,' Carmel replied. 'But as soon as you started having your fits when you were little, we knew we would have to go one day.'

'Oh.' Esme felt quite discombobulated. 'I thought you were happy here. That's why *I* never mentioned it.'

'Of course we're happy here, to a point,' Thomas said gently. 'But this country isn't safe for people like you. Why do you think we kept up the side business in the basement? We wanted to have money put aside so we could move to the Valley or the Kingdom of Mirrors before anything happened to you. Well.' He coughed. 'We also wanted to rebel against the queen.'

Esme sniffed, feeling oddly adrift. 'You did a good job of that.' Carmel laughed and gave her daughter a hug. She smelt like oregano and clean laundry.

'Before we make any decisions about moving anywhere, you should go to Laketown. Do your bit to put an end to all this nonsense with the Skeleton Rooms. You can pretend you're staying with my cousin. Everyone's noticed you have fits. We'll say that you've gone to speak to a physician.'

Esme nodded. 'That sounds like a plan. I'm not sure how long I'll be? It should take a couple of days to reach Laketown, maybe more, but I don't know what will happen when I get there. Violet wants to stay, but I don't know what her plans are exactly.'

There was a pause, and Esme realised she was waiting for her parents to tell her what would happen. Carmel just gave her another hug. 'You can't predict the future all the time, Esme. I will come with you if you ask me to, but I also think it's high time you got out of this inn and used those wits of yours.'

'I suppose Carmel's Inn wouldn't really work without Carmel, would it?' Esme felt a shiver of fear at leaving home without her parents, at going to another kingdom. The furthest she had ever been from the inn was about four villages along the Queen's Road.

'You'll be fine,' Thomas said quickly. 'It'll be an adventure. And you'll have Violet. Now, let's find you a decent stagecoach. I'm not having you travel on a dodgy public cart.'

Chapter Four

An hour later, standing in the inn's reception area, Esme hugged her parents tightly, a small pouch of money to bribe the guards in one hand, a falsified physician's referral letter in the other and a duffel bag over her shoulder. *It's only a few days*, she reminded herself. So why was the flutter in her stomach now a knot of dread?

'Good luck with the physician!' Thomas said loudly as he helped them into their approved stagecoach. 'I'm sure they'll be very helpful!' Esme managed to roll her eyes.

Carmel leaned into the carriage and pressed a pouch of coins into Violet's palm. 'For when you're in the Valley,' she murmured. 'Esme knows the address of my cousin and his family. They'll let you stay while you sort yourself out.'

Violet stepped out of the carriage and hugged Carmel for a full thirty seconds.

Twenty minutes later, their coach reached the checkpoint. Trying to ignore the resentful looks of foot travellers waiting their turn, Esme hopped out and approached the barrier. Up close, Esme noticed the guards had upgraded their uniform since the last time she was paying attention: as well as the standard sword and shield, each guard carried a truncheon, a length of chain and a wicked looking dagger on their belt. The cool day was abruptly colder.

Worse, Esme realised with a jolt that she knew the head guard on duty, Mr Garcia. He was her friend Georgiana's father. Esme was sure he would let them through without the need for a bribe, truncheon or not; his mother was a nurse at the local infirmary and helped keep Esme calm when her visions made her physically ill. The entire Garcia family kept her secret, and the Delacroix family repaid it by supplying one of Georgiana's aunts with a steady supply of potion equipment.

'You going south for a visit, Miss Esme?' Mr Garcia asked, peering down at the hastily forged letter and ignoring her pouch of coins. His face was almost hidden by his overstated helmet. At the next carriage along, one of his colleagues negotiated a bribe with a cheese merchant.

'Yes,' Esme replied. 'My father has asked me to go down the Queen's Road to our cousin. He wants me to see a specialist doctor about my fits.'

'Very nasty fits they are too, Miss Esme. Have a nice trip, I hope you find the help you need.' He helped her back into the carriage and before Esme had time to look back out of the window, they were in the Valley of Dreams.

It looked… exactly like the Queen's Road.

Violet stuck her head out of the window. 'We can make this go faster.'

'Can we? The horses are going pretty fast.'

Violet leaned further out of the coach, muttering. A moment later, the coach lurched forward, rattling over cobblestones.

'What did you do?' Esme asked, trying not to look impressed and failing. Exhilaration replaced her apprehension, just for a moment. 'You know, until this morning, I'd never actually seen anyone cast a spell.'

Violet grinned. Esme realised she hadn't seen Violet smile before. It suited her. 'I've been practising for ages. The horses have stopped moving entirely, not that anyone will notice anything different. I've manipulated the wind currents to propel us along.'

Esme raised an eyebrow. 'That'll teach me to underestimate the power of wind.'

Even with magic, their journey to Laketown was quicker than they expected, probably because the roads were quieter since the trade disputes began. That morning's newspaper had mentioned that the five-yearly sporting games between the three kingdoms would not be happening that summer. Esme wondered how long it would be before there was no reason for anyone to leave their own kingdom.

Arriving in Laketown after only a few quiet hours of flicking through Violet's notebook and studying the plans of the Skeleton Rooms, they wandered the city for a bit before stopping for lunch at one of the cafés by the spectacular lagoon. Esme drank in every sight, even though she had been right about the Valley and Stormhaven being quite similar. Everything looked alike… until she noticed the floating tea trays and merpeople and brightly coloured temples. Which god would she worship if she had the choice? All of them? None? She felt a hum of excitement in her chest. If she had an episode right here and now, would anyone notice?

'How are we going to get an audience with King Richard and Queen Florence?' Violet asked as they walked up to the White Palace. She looked more relaxed and healthier already, though she clutched her bag tightly. 'They aren't just going to let us in.'

Esme realised she hadn't thought that far ahead. So much for foresight.

'No uninvited visitors!' a guard told them when they reached the gate.

'It's important!' Esme argued.

'Everyone's issue is important,' the guard replied. 'You can make a request to visit King Richard in the public consultations. They take place on Monday and Wednesday afternoons.'

'It's about the Skeleton Rooms!' Esme said urgently. 'Please, we came from the Queen's Road—'

'Shall I enchant him?' Violet asked.

Before Esme had time to respond, a voice asked, 'Did you say you came from the Queen's Road?'

There was Queen Florence, holding a scruffy dog on a lead and resplendent in the nicest black lace gown Esme had ever seen, which was sad considering it clearly wasn't her fanciest gown. There wasn't a gem in sight.

'Yes, Your Majesty.' Esme bobbed into a hasty curtsey and hoped she was doing it correctly. 'I have the second sight, Your Majesty. We have important evidence about the Skeleton Rooms.'

'Come in. My husband and I cannot receive you, I'm afraid; we are about to have a meeting with the King and Queen of the Kingdom of Mirrors. But my son and his friends will see you.'

Esme was expecting a Great Hall with thrones, servants and several guards.

What she got was a Great Hall in which three teenagers were ignoring elegant High Council chairs in favour of tiny stools at a large chessboard.

Prince Richard and Princess Amelia scowled at the board while Prince George sat to one side, face amused. A sphere of fire floated lazily in his palm.

Esme coughed to announce their arrival. Amelia stood up and looked over the pair of them, as though trying to pull their thoughts from their skulls. She looked just like her portrait: tall, with wide brown eyes and afro hair pinned back with a clip. After a moment, she shook their hands warmly. Prince Richard followed her lead. Esme was surprised by the strength of his handshake; his portraits always depicted a chubby, awkward youth, alarmed by his royal status. This boy was stout and slightly ungainly, but he held himself with surprising confidence.

Only Prince George stayed back, shaking each of their hands briefly then retreating to the seat next to Richard. Esme found him almost difficult to look at: she had never seen anyone with blue eyes before. Beside her, she felt Violet's identical curiosity.

'Your Majesties,' Esme began. She wasn't sure who to look at, so she chose Amelia. 'My name is Esme Delacroix. This is Violet Beauchamp. I'm a seer. Violet's a—'

'A witch, Your Majesties.'

'We have evidence of Queen Margaret's cruelty and treachery.'

George muttered, 'So have I.' Richard elbowed him.

Esme drew the glass walnut from her pocket, hoping Esmeralda's spells had worked. Now it held her memories, it glowed blue. Even George eyed it with interest. Esme tapped it sharply until the sides split open and mist gurgled out, shapes forming in the air until Esme recognised the start of her vision.

Children, chained, shuffling through rain and sludge. Families sat on carts, huddled together. An enormous stone castle with plumes of black smoke spewing from large chimneys.

George leaned forward, the image of the castle dancing around his face like fog. 'Is that the Skeleton Rooms? Do you know where this is? Are you from the north of Stormhaven?'

Esme shook her head. 'I'm from the Queen's Road, Your Majesty, on the border. Until my vision, I didn't even know for certain if the Skeleton Rooms existed.'

Violet stepped forward. 'It's somewhere near Star's Point, Your Majesty. My father works there.' She placed her notebook and the prison plans on the chess board. The three royals examined them like they were museum pieces. Prince George flicked through Violet's diary and winced.

'May we keep all this?' he asked Violet. Violet looked alarmed but nodded. George stood up, agitated, and Esme thought she saw sparks fly from his hands.

'George?' Richard turned to his friend. 'I thought you didn't know anything about the Skeleton Rooms?'

'I don't—I didn't.' He pulled a face and threw himself back into his chair. 'My mother was from the north. From a hamlet near Star's Point. She used to tell me a story, to get me to behave… About a castle inhabited by demons that would find bad children and eat them.

'When I was older my mother told me that the folk tale was inspired by a real story, by the wars between the old clans. Apparently one of the lords used to have a castle he would use as a giant prisoner-of-war camp. I didn't make the connection until just now, but Miss Beauchamp's diary makes me doubtful the Skeleton Rooms are anywhere else.'

'I read about that lord in history class,' Amelia murmured.

Richard nodded. 'So did I. Marcel the Mad. He would use his prisoners' ashes to fertilise his vegetable garden. He had a whole set of rooms specifically for torturing and killing people. My parents wouldn't let me read all the books we have about him in case I had nightmares. I didn't know his castle was still standing… The Clan Wars happened hundreds of years ago.'

They all looked at the misty image, lingering over them like dust.

'Well.' Amelia broke the uncomfortable silence. 'Who would like a cup of tea? And a biscuit? I never consider court business on an empty stomach.'

Esme collapsed the walnut and stowed it in her pocket, the mist dissipating like steam from a kettle. George put Violet's journal and parchment under a chair. They all seemed glad to be rid of them.

'I recognise the name Beauchamp,' Amelia said to Violet as she poured tea. 'Is your family from the Kingdom of Mirrors?'

'My mother's from the Valley, near Charmedwater Canal… my father came from Lumiere. They met at university in the Valley and went back to Lumiere together. We moved to Stormhaven Town when I was small.'

'When exactly did you leave Lumiere?' Amelia asked.

Violet sipped tea. 'Just after the Midsummer Riots.'

'If I were to look your father up, would I find his name on a list of people who engineered the riots?'

'Almost definitely.' Violet gripped her teacup. 'I can give you his address if you like—'

Something pulled the air from Esme's lungs. *Not now*, she thought desperately—

She vaguely felt herself slump in her chair. Somewhere someone was saying, *'Are you all right?'* but she was already in a very different royal palace:

Queen Margaret sat on her throne, looking more like her statue in Esme's village square than an actual person. Margaret was in her seventies, possibly older, and had ruled for so long that few could remember a time before her reign. The woman glaring down from her throne looked as though she knew this and used it to her advantage. Her high nose and heavy eyebrows were accentuated by a tight bun of grey hair, pulling her olive skin taut and making her even sterner. About twelve rings glinted on her fingers, which gripped her throne like a vice. Her outfit was more regal than any of the clothes Esme had seen other royals wearing: a high-necked dress in a silvery material, embroidered with thousands of pearls.

It looked as though it would fit in at a wedding, state dinner, or funeral. Margaret's gaze was on a small child, hunched on the rug in front of her throne. Tear tracks stained his face.

'What was its crime?' she asked.

Esme heard a guard somewhere out of the picture say, 'We found it levitating its toys.'

Margaret surveyed the child as though contemplating a boil on her foot.

'Take it to the Skeleton Rooms. Get it out of my sight.'

Large arms picked the child up and swept him from the room as he cried, the sound echoing off the cold walls.

Margaret turned to speak to someone else, and Esme realised with a thrill that she recognised him from newspaper illustrations: it was the Duke of Stormhaven Town, rumoured to have masterminded the Eaton Plot.

'This is getting out of hand,' Margaret snapped. 'Why are so many of them flaunting their abilities?'

The duke shifted his weight. 'It might be something to do with your nephew, Your Majesty—'

'*Do not mention that child to me,*' Margaret hissed. 'He is a blot on the history of this kingdom.' She took a deep breath to compose herself, obsidian eyes glinting in the lamplight. 'Do the other kingdoms move against us in response to their little refugee crisis?'

'For that to happen, Your Majesty, they would have to know exactly what's causing it.'

'Are we absolutely sure that they don't?' Margaret pressed. 'I do not want my plans uncovered before we've had a chance to put all our affairs into order.'

The duke laughed. 'The Mad Prince hasn't set foot here for nearly a decade. King Richard and Queen Florence haven't visited for almost as long. The last time we saw Emmanuel and Hazel, that daughter of theirs was still in primary school. No one has ever escaped the Skeleton Rooms, and all the migrants can say with honesty is that there are *rumours* of something going on. No one in the Three Kingdoms will start a war because of rumours, ma'am. All Laketown and Lumiere know is that people are moving south. And who could blame them, with the cruel trade restrictions recently placed on Stormhaven?'

Margaret considered. 'What are we doing to stop the cockroaches leaving in the first place?'

'Border control has been stepped up, Your Majesty. We know people are still getting through, probably bribing officials and paying smugglers to get them across. We have appealed to King Richard to tighten his side of the border, but we have not yet had a response.'

'Write again,' Margaret commanded, 'and reiterate the danger these people pose to his community. His kingdom was already swamped by foreigners once—you really think he wants to be overrun again? And by people with such violent, disgusting predilections?'

'I'll do it now, Your Majesty.' The duke nodded and turned to leave.

'Wait!' Margaret called him back. 'Doesn't that disgraced Duke of Lumiere still live on Traveller's End Mountain with some goatherd or other?'

'Yes, ma'am, although latest intelligence suggests that they aren't getting along.'

'Really? Why?'

'Prince Nicholas spent a lot of last summer with his sister,' the duke recalled. 'There were whispers of them arguing in public about the husband.'

The Queen looked thoughtful. 'Send a scout to inspect the farm. I want to make sure it's complying with all regulations. Should anything be out of place, I want to know about it.'

'Yes ma'am.' He bowed and swept from the room.

Esme's vision cleared and she remembered where she was. Four faces peered down at her. Not the impression she had hoped to make on royalty…

'What was that?' Amelia looked alarmed.

'That,' Esme said as Violet helped her sit up, 'was my magic.'

Instead of recounting her vision, Esme dug the walnut from her pocket and performed the spell the witch had taught her, so they could see for themselves.

'That's a lot of detail,' George commented when the mist faded.

'I think it's clearer if I do the spell straight away,' Esme muttered. She felt slightly lightheaded from watching the scene twice.

'Do you know how far in advance your visions are?' Richard asked.

'I had one recently that was almost instantaneous,' Esme admitted. 'I've never fully tested it. I'm quite good at predicting who's going to win the lottery in our village, and that usually happens about a week after I've seen it. I think the longest gap between a vision and the vision happening is…' She thought about it. 'Maybe six weeks? I had a vision about the summer solstice festival once, about six weeks before it happened.'

'I'm fairly sure our magicians could tell you more,' Richard leant forward. 'I know some of them have made it their life's work to research the second sight. Have you ever spoken to a magician before?'

'No. We don't have magicians in Stormhaven.' Esme knew her voice was bitter. She looked at the floor.

'Well, if you ever want to learn some more, you know where we are.' Richard's easy tone made Esme feel worse.

Amelia hadn't spoken since Esme came back from her vision. She kept tapping against her cup.

'Are you all right?' Violet asked.

'My brother could be in danger.' Amelia looked ill. 'Could they really be employing the same methods as Marcel the Mad? That would mean the most horrific deaths…' she trailed off, eyes somewhere else. 'Gods, we need to warn him!' She paused, as if realising that she made very little sense to her companions. 'Nicholas is a magic user,' she said quietly. She rubbed her eyes and turned her face away. 'It's not long until dinner. Let's speak to our parents.'

An hour or so later, both sets of monarchs had seen Esme's visions. If she hadn't been magically showing them the inside of her head, Esme would have been shaking with excitement to share a meal with the four most important people in the Three Kingdoms. They all greeted Esme and Violet with warm handshakes and offers of rooms for the night, which was more hospitality than Esme had encountered from the entire government of Stormhaven in her fourteen years of living there.

An uneasy silence settled over the room once Esme had tucked the walnut back into her pocket. Their food lay forgotten.

'Well,' said Queen Hazel.

'Quite,' murmured Queen Florence.

'Not good,' King Emmanuel sighed.

'Not good at all,' King Richard agreed.

'I think we need to ask Nicholas to come home,' Queen Hazel said, eyes on her husband. She looked up at the room. 'We have not heard from our son, the Duke of Lumiere, for several weeks. I didn't think much of it until I saw your vision, Miss Delacroix. He was looking into the rumours of the Skeleton Rooms.' She tapped the table. 'It's entirely possible he's being held prisoner.'

King Richard sat forward. 'We need more evidence of what Miss Delacroix saw in her vision before we can act—and then we must decide *how* we should act. This sort of treatment of civilians by a monarch is unprecedented. I did not think we would see Marcel the Mad's castle in use again, let alone that it would turn out to be the same place we've been hearing whispers of for months.'

'Why don't I go up to the Skeleton Rooms?' Esme asked suddenly.

'You?' asked George, turning his icy eyes onto her.

'Yes, me,' Esme said defensively. 'I'm the only person here with easy access to the Queen's Road, since I live there. I can do magic. I wouldn't need to be at the castle for long, only enough time to see what's going on. I could… get myself arrested.' As she said it, Esme realised the gravity of what she was suggesting. What was she doing, volunteering to go to the Skeleton Rooms? Had she hit her head when she fell in the kitchen?

'It could help us learn whatever Margaret is up to.' Prince Richard pushed his glasses up his nose with a sideways glance at Esme. 'I think it's a good idea. She's right, George, she's the only one of us with a good excuse to go to Stormhaven—and she's already proven that she's brave enough to come down here.' He smiled faintly at Esme. 'Besides, Margaret said something about *uncovering plans.* That sounds… ominous.'

'More ominous than the mass imprisonment of magic users? What could be worse?' Amelia asked.

'Unrest in Stormhaven as people suffer from the trade barriers we've imposed,' Queen Florence replied. She picked at a piece of lace on her sleeve. 'Which could lead to riots. A civil war, perhaps. Or war between the kingdoms. And knowing what that castle was used for? I would not be surprised to find a genocide of magic users.'

'Genocide? You think it could be that bad?' Prince Richard looked at his mother in alarm.

Florence shrugged. 'You know your history books, Richard. Nothing ends well when a country begins imprisoning one particular group of its citizens.'

'But even if we do find out what Margaret's planning, can we stop her?' Amelia asked. 'And by 'we', I literally mean the combined military and magical forces of the two kingdoms….' she rubbed her temples. 'I feel as though if witnessing a genocide is the worst possible outcome of all this, then war with Margaret could be the best possible outcome. Which would be… awful.'

'Miss Delacroix, are you absolutely sure about going to the Skeleton Rooms?' Queen Hazel did not carry herself with the same confidence her daughter did, although they had the same expressions.

'You need me to go and collect evidence,' Esme said. Richard's comments had fortified her, just a little. 'I can go where you can't.'

'Can you do the hologram walnut trick with memories?' King Richard asked. 'Or is it just visions?'

'It's all thoughts.' Esme confirmed. 'So, to collect evidence of Margaret's treachery, I should go north, get arrested and sent to the Skeleton Rooms, watch what's happening for a day or so, then return here with evidence so you can decide what to do about it?'

'There's one more thing,' Hazel said. 'Our son and son-in-law live on Traveller's End Mountain. It's not far from the Queen's Road. Could you…'

'I'll stop there and find out what's happened. If I can, I'll bring them both back here with me.'

'Thank you.'

'I'll come too.' Violet hadn't spoken for at least ten minutes. 'I have magic that's more obvious than yours, so I can get us arrested easily. Also, I've studied this.' She tugged the castle plan from her bag and set it on the table. 'My father works in the Skeleton Rooms. As a… I'm not sure. But I can help. And you shouldn't go there alone.'

'Are you sure?' Esme asked. 'You didn't want to go back to Stormhaven. Your father's colleagues might recognise you.'

Violet looked uncomfortable when she realised she had the room's attention. 'This is important. Anyway, it will only be a few days.'

'What if you get caught?' Queen Florence asked. 'I'm not having you go anywhere near the prison if there's no way for us to find you if something goes wrong.'

'What about a tracking spell?' George suggested. 'They're not precise over long distances, but they're better than nothing. They would allow us to get a better idea of where the Skeleton Rooms are too.'

Florence looked as though she would rather arm Esme and Violet with flares and a collapsible bodyguard, but she nodded her assent.

Esme prodded her food. Get back across the border, visit Traveller's End Mountain, hope that it didn't end her particular journey, reach the Skeleton Rooms, collect some evidence about potential atrocities, pick up a couple of dukes on the way and come back in one piece.

It seemed about as easy as doing magic in Stormhaven, which was to say that it might kill her, but she was going to do it anyway.

'How will we travel?' she asked. 'On horseback or by carriage, the journey from here to Star's Point will take weeks.'

'Not in our carriages it won't,' Queen Hazel said. 'We can lend you the royal carriage and our coachman. Disguised, of course.'

'We can provide you with some tricks to make everything easier,' Queen Florence added quickly. 'An invisibility bracelet will help you sneak around the castle. Hazel is excellent at protection spells. George, do you have anything magical close at hand?'

'Yes, ma'am.' George looked delighted to have been asked. 'I think I have something lying around.'

Chapter Five

At dawn the next day, Esme and Violet departed with a hug from Amelia and Richard and a handshake from their parents. Prince George just handed them a small stack of magical objects and performed a couple of tracking spells, which involved dousing them in yellow dust and muttering for five minutes. Esme hadn't slept much, although the bed she had been given was so soft she could have been lying on a cloud. They left their bags in their rooms, only taking what could fit in the pockets of their clothes. *I'm coming back in a few days*, Esme reminded herself. *Then I'm going home.*

The Lumiere stagecoach made Violet's trick with the horses look like a parlour game. This carriage zoomed along like a racing boat. Snug inside, driven by a wizened old gentleman named Albertine, Esme and Violet could have been on their way to the hot spring for a holiday.

George had given them vials of his feature-changing potion, so they could get in and out of the Skeleton Rooms with relative ease, but when they reached the Queen's Road border they passed through as themselves. Georgiana's dad waved them through with a smile. 'Back so soon, Miss Esme. How was the physician?'

'Very useful, thank you. A worthwhile journey.'

On the other side of the border the queue had swelled in just a couple of days. Where there had been hundreds of families, now Esme was sure she could have counted to one thousand.

'The rumours are spreading,' Violet said quietly. 'No one wants to risk the Skeleton Rooms.'

Some travellers held signs with hand-painted slogans such as '*HELL-haven*,' '*The Gods Are Watching, Margaret*' and '*FIGHT FOR YOUR MAGICAL RIGHTS*.' As they passed, one guard wrestled a placard from a protester and handcuffed her roughly. Esme looked away.

The line of travellers reached long past Carmel's Inn, stretching almost too far to see. Esme had Albertine stop the coach so they could see her parents, who seemed older than they had two days ago. They aged further when Esme explained what they were planning. 'I don't like it,' Carmel said over lunch. She heaped food on to Violet and Esme's plates, as though an extra helping of hummus would make their journey easier. 'I don't like it *at all*. Going down to the Valley by yourself is one thing, but—you're children. Violet, I can't stop you, but Esme—'

'You could *try* to stop me. Anyway, you were the one who said I should use my wits.'

Carmel hissed and rattled crockery.

'Are you sure about this?' Thomas scowled. 'I know you're capable, Esme, but I think they should send someone else. Someone older.'

'We're both sure,' Esme said. 'If Princess Amelia can defeat the Sapphire Dragon, we can do a little reconnaissance trip.' Esme had not shared with her parents the uglier details of her visions: she knew they would panic and worry, which would make her panic and worry. She also wanted to be sure that if it all went wrong and her parents were arrested, neither of them could give anything away even under the influence of truth dust.

'People queuing at the border are getting restless,' Thomas continued after a moment. 'The guards keep throwing their weight around. I wouldn't be surprised if we have another version of the Midsummer Riots before long.'

'That might be just what Margaret wants,' Carmel said quietly.

Violet and Esme left the inn after lunch. Esme hugged both her parents fiercely. 'Be careful,' her mother told her, her arms digging into Esme's shoulders. She hugged Violet too. 'Mind the roads.' She stepped back from the path and called, 'Enjoy your trip to Stormhaven Town!' This time, Violet rolled her eyes as well.

Albertine turned the coach west as soon as they were out of sight of the border crossing, heading toward Traveller's End Mountain. Within hours they were on such narrow roads the carriage had trouble turning corners. They stopped for the night, hiding the coach under a camouflage blanket on the side of the road. Someone had bewitched the interior to include a little bathroom, a basket of food, some blankets and several toothbrushes. Esme loved magic.

'I have an idea,' Violet said once Albertine was snoring gently in the seat next to her. 'In case one of us gets caught at the Skeleton Rooms. Or both of us, actually.'

'Go on?'

Violet told her.

'No.'

'Esme, we need a continuity plan.'

'That is a suicide mission, not a continuity plan.'

'Not necessarily. Just think about it.'

The next day Esme woke at sunrise, disorientated. She had dreamt—something. Next to her, Violet was breathing deeply, her hair over her face like a veil. Or a shroud. *Continuity plans.* Esme scowled, pushed away the thought and went to brush her teeth.

After breakfast, leaving Albertine to tend to the horses, Esme and Violet hiked along the path on foot, following a map Amelia had drawn. A spring shower became a spring storm within minutes. Before they knew it, they were battling mud, hailstones, and a wind that tried to gouge out their eyes. Gradually, the path became so steep they could have climbed it. Esme tried and failed to think of a more apt name for the mountain.

Hours later, the downpour had just begun to ease up when they found themselves on a tiny terrace in front of a single-storey stone building. Amelia's directions must have been sound, because there were dozens of goats wandering around.

'Hello?' Esme called. 'Your Highness? Your Highnesses?'

'Who are you?' called a man's rough voice from inside the building.

'Are you Nicholas or Raphael?' Esme asked cautiously.

'Who's asking?'

'My name is Esme Delacroix. I'm a seer. I've been sent by your sister—by Amelia.'

'Prove it!'

'The scar on Nicholas' foot is from a chess game when he was eight. It needed twelve stitches because Amelia upended the entire chessboard when she lost.' Esme hoped she had remembered Amelia's anecdote correctly.

The wooden front door opened and a grubby, olive face poked out. Too light skinned to be Nicholas, but scruffier than in his portraits, this must be Raphael.

'Nicholas has gone.'

Esme appreciated his candour but wished he would leave his door. 'Raphael, sir, please may we come in? I don't think it's safe to be out here for long.'

Raphael's head disappeared and a moment later, the door opened fully. Stepping over the threshold, Esme was reminded both of her parents' inn and paintings of Lumiere. The house—well, it was a hut—had only two rooms, but almost every surface was covered in bright paint, a mirror or a mosaic. Richly embroidered rugs covered the floor and a small shrine sat in one corner, a couple of candles burning happily. The practical part of the home was all Stormhaven: a dark wood bed with heavy cotton blankets, several pairs of thick leather boots at the front door and a general, lingering smell of animal. Raphael made tea and hung their jackets up to dry while Esme explained their journey to the Skeleton Rooms and why they had come to the mountain.

'Nicholas has gone,' he repeated, setting a tray on the little table. He cleared two ancient chairs of prayer books, gestured at the girls to sit down and poured tea.

'How long ago did he leave? Or was he taken?' Esme asked.

Raphael leant on the sideboard. 'He set off about six weeks ago. Ever since he came back from Princess Amelia's festival, he was worried about what's happening to magic users. We asked around and he got wind of where the prison is. He said he wanted to go and see it for himself.'

'And you just let him go?' Violet asked incredulously. Raphael frowned. Esme reminded herself that Violet was not used to relationships in which one person respected the other person's wishes.

'I am not his keeper. Nicholas thought he would be protected by his status.'

'Have you heard from him at all?' Esme asked.

'I had a message by carrier pigeon about five days after he left saying he had reached Star's Point.'

'That was quick,' Violet remarked. 'That sort of journey should take weeks.'

'He's become quite good at bewitching things.' Raphael said. He sounded grudgingly proud.

'How was he planning to infiltrate the prison?'

'Get himself arrested, maybe. Or use an enchantment. I don't think he had a plan.' He scowled at the floor. 'I was going to give it a few more days then go and find him myself. There have been... we've heard... I wasn't sure what to do. It's hard to leave the farm,' he added, as though they were questioning why he hadn't left already. 'It's a lot of work. And I'm not a soldier.' He scowled again.

Esme sipped tea. 'Please consider coming back to Laketown with us after we're done at the Skeleton Rooms, then carry on down to Lumiere. Even—even if we don't find him there.'

'Why?'

Esme swallowed. How much information would be enough to persuade him to leave with them, and how much would worry him further? 'We've seen, um, evidence about what's happening at the Skeleton

Rooms. It's not safe for magic users in Stormhaven anymore. Your family want you both on safe ground. Please.'

Raphael exhaled loudly. Esme counted the colours on the walls. Violet gazed at the shrine in the corner.

'Could I bring the goats?'

'Maybe. Hopefully! We'll figure something out.'

Figuring something out meant Violet casting a shrinking spell over the entire herd, which was rounded up with surprising speed by Raphael, and placing every goat into a single grass-lined crate. For good measure, Violet shrank everything in the hut that wasn't nailed down and packed it all into a wooden trunk. Esme wondered if she would ever get bored of watching magic happen in front of her very eyes.

'I'm not coming back here, am I?' Raphael asked quietly. He twisted the wedding ring on his finger and stared at the empty room.

'Probably not any time soon,' Esme admitted. 'But I'm going to bring Nicholas back from the Skeleton Rooms. I promise.'

'Don't say that,' Raphael said flatly. He watched Violet levitate the trunk with narrowed eyes. 'You shouldn't make promises you can't keep.'

He led them down the muddy mountain track in silence, carrying the goat crate on his shoulder.

The Skeleton Rooms were some three hundred miles away, but Albertine's coach covered the distance overnight. When they first saw the castle from the carriage, it was the size of a postage stamp. A few hours later, it was the size of the palace at Laketown. Even from a great distance, it was a grim sight: an obsidian shadow, somehow bigger than the colossal mountains surrounding it.

The nearest proper town to the Skeleton Rooms was Star's Point, dozens of miles south, but a few tiny hamlets dotted around the landscape, cowering in the mountains' shadows. They chose a cluster of huts at random, several miles from the castle. Esme felt as though the air was holding its breath, somehow, as if the atmosphere itself was on edge. As Albertine pulled up the coach, she felt as nauseous as she did after an episode.

'We will wait for you right outside the castle gate, camouflaged,' Albertine told them. 'If you do not come back through the gates within thirty-six hours, we come to find you.'

Raphael did not look happy about being left behind, but he nodded, twisting his wedding ring as though it itched. 'Are you absolutely sure I shouldn't come with you?'

'You're a member of the Kingdom of Mirrors' royal family,' Esme reminded him. 'We can't risk something happening to you too.'

'Four years ago I was just a farmer. Sometimes I think that was the easier life.' He scowled. 'I'll pray for you.'

'Thank you,' Esme said, hoping she sounded braver than she felt. This high up, the wind was harsh and biting. Esme wished they had thought to wear thicker coats, instead of jackets over woollen trousers. She wished they had thought to bring backup. She wished she had thought to tell her parents she loved them.

'Right. Let's get arrested.'

Chapter Six

Breaking into the Skeleton Rooms turned out to be the easy part. With George's disguise potion applied liberally to their faces and more concealed within their clothes, plus a couple of invisibility bracelets ('use them sparingly, the magic wears off after a few hours,') and some vials ('do not drop these under any circumstances,') Violet conjured a purple flame. She hurled it into the air, transforming it into a glowing orb that floated down to Esme, who kicked it back to Violet. They soon had an energetic game, which Violet encouraged by levitating them both several feet into the air. Esme found herself laughing as she lunged through the air, clawing at the orb as though she were playing with a ball in the swimming baths on the Queen's Road. Across from her, Violet was flushed with exertion and almost crying with laughter. 'You're supposed to *kick* it—'

'Hey! Get down from there!' Ten or so heavily armed men wearing Queen Margaret's coat of arms appeared from the trees. They pulled the girls down, cuffing their hands behind their backs.

'Names?'

'Tallulah Pinkerton,' Violet muttered, now every bit the sulky teenager. She was disguised as someone from the Kingdom of Mirrors, with umber skin and an afro. Esme's eyes were brown, her mousy curls now rather like Violet's chestnut hair.

'Harriet Smith,' Esme said. 'Where are you taking us?' she called to the soldiers, mindful that she needed to collect as much evidence as possible.

'Nowhere you'll come back from,' one of the soldiers said nastily. His colleague rapped him on the shoulder.

'Hey, we've been told not to say anything,' he said. 'Queen's orders.'

'It's not as though they'll get out, though, is it?' The first soldier smirked. 'None of these little insects will see the light of day again.'

'Don't call us that!' Violet snapped. 'We're just people—'

Almost faster than Esme could watch, the soldier struck her over the head with the butt of his sword. Violet hit the ground so violently that

161

Esme heard something crack. Esme contorted her bound arms to help Violet to her feet, biting back her fury. A line of blood trickled over Violet's eye and one of her knees looked incorrect, somehow, like it was on the wrong way round. She wobbled as she stood, breathing heavily. Before either of them could say anything, they were pulled onto an open cart and covered with an old burlap sack.

The cart was moving within seconds, trundling along at speed but not in the direction of the castle. As the day wore on, Violet muttered something, freed her arms and strapped up her knee with a piece of cloth torn from her jacket, before clicking the cuffs back on. Esme realised that the soldiers' entire job entailed driving from hamlet to hamlet arresting magic users, based on tip-offs delivered by carrier pigeon. At each stop they collected more prisoners. At nightfall they were no closer to the Skeleton Rooms but had stopped at six other dwellings, all of which held magic users of some description.

'I was only casting a protection spell on my children—' one prisoner told her captors.

'My house was falling down, and I needed to repair it,' an elderly man pleaded. 'It was just a simple fixing spell. Please, I would have nowhere to live otherwise.'

They spent the night in the carts, crammed in together, allowed off only to use some questionable public lavatories. Esme and Violet reapplied the disguise potion, although the soldiers paid them so little attention it was unlikely they would notice if the queen had stepped onto the cart. Dinner consisted of what Esme thought was probably supposed to be soup. It looked like something from inside the lavatories.

Early the next morning, the convoy picked up eight more people, the youngest of whom was no more than six. In the dawn light, Violet looked horrendous: a new bruise had spread over the right side of her face and dried blood was stuck to her hair. Underneath her trousers, her injured knee was twice the size of the other. The cart was uncomfortably full and impossibly cold even with all the prisoners huddled inside. Esme hadn't realised that fear had a smell. No one spoke. Violet leant on her.

Esme realised she had dozed off when the cart stopped suddenly and jolted her awake.

In front of them loomed the Skeleton Rooms.

Up close it was even uglier, leaning over them like a hurricane. Esme counted nine turrets and no windows. Each prisoner was pulled out of the cart, handcuffed to the person next to them and pushed into a line of people that ran up several steep steps and through an enormous stone door.

The soldiers left in their carts. The queue shuffled along at a snail's pace. Guards stood at the stone door, impossibly still.

Violet was trembling, leaning heavily on Esme with half-closed eyes. Esme glanced at the sky. It was black with storm clouds. She glanced back at the gates. Just past them was a copse of trees that could, potentially, resemble a stagecoach and horses.

Someone passed out further along the queue. A guard scraped them up and pushed them back into line. More soldiers brought more prisoners.

Esme's stomach growled with hunger. The monotony was almost as bad as the fear. Their disguises were almost completely faded. But then, up here, no one cared what they looked like. If Violet were recognised by a guard, would it really matter? Esme doubted the staff here were trained to care who they arrested.

Hours later, they reached the steps. A few more hours and they were through the door into a sprawling, draughty entrance hall. Esme knew from the architect's plans that the hall took up most of the castle's ground floor. Their handcuffs were removed and handed to a fresh contingent of soldiers, heading out on an empty cart. Clearly, no one expected them to try to escape.

One pair of guards stood at the top of the hall, with more at the walls. The line reminded Esme of the queue for the border back at home: at least five hundred people stood waiting, except here they were hemmed in by little chain-link barriers. Some looked exhausted; others bore fresh injuries. There were small children, elderly people, groups of families. Some were dressed like locals, in thick cloaks and boots. Others looked as though they lived closer to the Queen's Road, wearing thinner clothing and huddling together. Esme scanned the room, taking in entire families, couples clinging to one another and—there he was. The toddler from her vision, maybe thirty people ahead of them. He was whimpering, looking up at the hall through thick eyelashes. His little jumper was torn and he seemed to be missing one of his shoes. Esme wondered who his parents were, and where they were. She was relieved when a teenage boy next to him scooped him up and rocked him gently. Next to her, Violet swayed and Esme wrapped both arms around her. She wasn't sure who was keeping who upright. A guard glowered at them.

After a few more minutes of watching, Esme realised they were in some sort of testing room. Ironically, it looked as though they were using magical means to discern magic users. When a prisoner reached the front of the queue at the other end of the hall, they were directed to stand in the middle of a chalk circle. After a few seconds, the circle lit up in coloured flame. If the fire glowed green, the prisoner was taken back toward the exit. Esme wondered if they were released, but she remembered the soldier saying, 'no one ever gets out of there.' Maybe they were thrown to wolves.

If the flame circle burnt purple, the prisoner was taken through an unmarked wooden door set into the stone wall. Esme did not want to think about what happened on the other side of the door. Still, nobody said anything. It was as though the castle had removed everyone's ability to speak. Esme did some calculations in her head. They were at the very back of the queue, and it looked as though one person was tested every thirty seconds or so. That meant they had about four hours before they reached the magic circles.

It was time to look around.

Violet was in no state to sneak about the castle. 'Stay here.' Esme breathed in her ear, as loudly as she dared. The guard glared at them, so Esme enveloped Violet in a hug, hoping they just looked scared and desperate, and kept talking. 'In one hour's time, put your invisibility bangle on and wait by the door we came in by. If I'm not back in three hours, run for it. Um. Hobble.'

Violet's face was a blotchy mess, one eye slightly swollen. Esme wondered how much injury a human head could take before the damage was permanent.

'Try downstairs to look for Nicholas,' she murmured. A small part of Esme marvelled that she could still notice Violet's violet smell, even now. 'It's where Marcel used to keep prisoners. Go as far down as you can.' She winced and shifted her weight from one leg to the other. 'I think I know a couple of spells that could interfere with those circles and confuse the guards. I'll do what I can to stall the queue.'

'Are you strong enough to do magic? Your leg needs looking at.'

'My dad threw me down a flight of stairs once. This isn't that bad. You also need a distraction. Leave it to me.' She squeezed Esme's hand then pitched forward in a faint.

'Help!' Esme called loudly. 'Help! My friend's collapsed! She won't be any good to anyone dead on the floor!' A guard stepped forward reluctantly as prisoners made space to let him through. Hoping the faint really was phony, Esme ducked behind a large man and slipped her invisibility bracelet onto her wrist. She waved a hand in front of her face to check the charm worked, then hopped over the barrier and out into the corridor.

Esme's first port of call was the guards' office. She knew it was unlikely that there would be a document on the desk entitled 'EVIL PLANS' but she also knew how easy it was for careless workers to leave information lying around; Esme's mother had once accidentally left details of a surprise birthday party in a shopping bag, and the recipient of the party (her father) had surprised her with a marriage proposal.

Esme slithered into the office when one of the guards went out to make tea and the other was engaged in the hallway, yelling at a colleague for showing sympathy to a prisoner. The desk was annoyingly empty except for a pack of sandwiches, and she didn't dare open drawers for risk of making noise. Someone had hung spare chainmail and a helmet on the hook on the back of the door. Her eyes fell on the wastepaper bin, full of rolled up parchments. She knelt down and rifled through as quietly as she could. She knew her memories would be viewed entirely by the High Councils of Laketown and Lumiere, so she tried to read as much as she could. Most of it made no sense. A prisoner clean up policy, minimum prisoner numbers, a map noting the areas of Stormhaven someone thought most full of magic users. They all looked like basic administrative instructions from the higher-ups. Useful, but Esme knew she needed more.

She hurried to a wooden cabinet just as the guards' argument reached fever pitch, risked opening it and seized a couple of documents. One folder was labelled 'ARMY ORGANISATION PLANS.' Another read 'QUEEN'S ROAD TO LAKETOWN.' She opened it to find more maps. Someone had annotated hiding places, vantage points and escape routes. She read as fast as she could, hoping the walnut's magic had a slow-motion replay option.

It would have to do. She replaced the documents, shut the cabinet and narrowly avoided colliding with the guard who returned with two steaming mugs of tea. Next stop: whatever was behind the door in the testing room.

Esme snuck back into the hall easily and searched for Violet. She was upright and leaning on another prisoner, but she didn't look as though the faint had been particularly difficult to fake.

Esme crept past the prisoners and up to the door at the very end of the hall, darting through it just as a guard came out of it. He was carrying a bag full of what looked like wooden figurines.

At first, it just looked like a smallish room. Then Esme noticed small heaps of ash, each sat at intervals of a few centimetres. The ceiling seemed to stretch on forever, until Esme realised she was looking up into one of the castle chimneys. She was standing inside an enormous fireplace. The door opened behind her and she leapt back, shrinking into the wall. There was nowhere to hide, so she had to hope no one would brush past her. The room filled slowly, a prisoner entering every thirty seconds or so from the magic circles. Everyone was holding a wooden figurine. They reminded her of Violet's doll. After about half an hour, the room was packed full and stuffy with terror. The door closed.

Before Esme had time to think, a blinding light swept through the chamber. She closed her eyes. When she opened them a second later, she was completely alone.

New piles of ash sat where the prisoners had stood a minute ago. The dolls sat next to them.

Two guards came in. One collected up the figurines while the other swept the ash into their dustpan.

Chapter Seven

Esme found a bathroom and vomited for about ten minutes after she slipped out of the room. *Room* was not quite the word. Execution chamber? Human furnace? She wiped her mouth and looked in the mirror, then remembered she was still wearing her invisibility bracelet. She had been gone about forty-five minutes: that left three hours at most before Violet reached the front of the queue if she hadn't slipped away to their meeting place. Esme nearly threw up again. They needed to leave, now.

But where was Prince Nicholas? If he had been taken to the furnace when he first arrived, his ashes would be long gone. Esme thought it more likely that Queen Hazel was right, that he had been taken prisoner. Heeding Violet's advice, she strode down flights of stairs until the air smelt dank and the ground felt more like soil than tiles. The guards seemed to have disappeared and the sounds of the castle above were muffled.

After a few minutes the staircase ended but the corridor ahead continued, so Esme kept going, still heading downwards. Passageways led on to passageways in a maze, but only one seemed lit by torchlight, so she followed it for what felt like an age. How far below the castle was she? Why was no one else around?

Esme only knew she had found the right room when the torches stopped. A door stood ajar: odd. There were no guards: odder. Feeling like she was back in the inn with Violet, she inched round the door.

Esme had expected chains or ropes, perhaps, to stop him escaping. Or maybe a nice cell with a bed frame and a waste bucket, as he was royalty. What she got was an emaciated man huddled in dirty travelling clothes, completely alone, eyes tightly shut. His bones stood out on his arms, clumps of hair were missing and there was a steady stream of blood seeping from his nose to his torn shirt. If he hadn't worn Amelia's face or the same silver wedding ring as Raphael, Esme would not have thought it possible that this could be the Prince Nicholas, Duke of Lumiere. He had been missing for a few weeks, not a few years. Could he be exaggerating his fatigue in order to gain sympathy with the guards?

Esme pulled off her bracelet. 'Nicholas? Your Majesty?'

His eyes opened. They were unfocused and sunken. 'Who are you?' His voice was raspy, and he could barely lift his head.

'My name is Esme Delacroix. Your sister sent me.'

'Amelia? Is she all right?'

'She was in perfect health a couple of days ago. She and your parents sent me to fetch you and Raphael.'

'How is he?'

'Extremely stressed. But fine.' Esme hesitated. Should she tell him Raphael was waiting on the other side of the gates? He looked like a shock would knock him out. 'How... what are you doing, exactly?'

The duke sat up with some difficulty. 'I think it's a forcefield of some sort. I was captured near Star's Point. One of the soldiers recognised me and they kicked me unconscious. When I came to, I was in here, locked in. But when guards came to interrogate me, no one seemed able to get past the door. I mean, they all literally bounced off the door frame. Except you.'

'Interesting.' The duke's breathing was laboured, like he couldn't catch his breath. Esme remembered Prince George, chalky white and skinny, and her nausea after every episode. Perhaps magic ate away at you, if you did it too much. 'Do you think you could keep up the forcefield if I helped you walk?'

'Maybe.'

'Right, then, we're getting out of here.' She edged forward and helped him up gingerly. He leant on her, lighter than Violet. 'There's a carriage waiting outside,' she said as he stumbled forward, like a lamb learning to walk. 'There's someone I've got to get, then we just have to reach the gates.'

'How?'

'I have just enough magic to disguise you between here and there, but we have to hurry.' She sprinkled the last of the potion on his head then slipped her bracelet back on. The magic did absolutely nothing to hide his wounds but lengthened his hair and lightened his skin enough that, if you were squinting, you might not recognise him as the man from the dungeon.

Esme had no idea how long it took them to get up the stairs and back to the entrance hall. She realised belatedly that Nicholas looked rather like he was leaning on air, and that neither she nor Violet could see one another. Why hadn't she thought to ask Queen Hazel for a spare invisibility bracelet? She propped Nicholas against a wall out of sight of the guards and hurried across the hall to the meeting place.

'Violet?' she hissed. A guard stood not ten feet away, eyes on the queue of prisoners.

'Here,' said a voice. It sounded weak, but Esme felt the air until she had hold of Violet's hand. 'Did you find what we needed?'

'Yep. Did you cast any spells?'

'Yep.'

'Then let's go.' On the way back to Nicholas, Esme flitted into the guards' office and grabbed the chainmail and helmet. Back where she left the prince, he was breathing loudly and wobbled a little when he pulled the armour over his head. Nobody with sense would be fooled, but nobody with sense would work somewhere with a human fireplace, so maybe they could reach the gates unnoticed.

One day, Esme reflected as she navigated the queue and led her companions to the front door, an invisible person leading a seriously ill person and an invisible seriously ill person across a packed hall would make quite a funny comedy sketch. Today was not that day. Violet and Esme managed to hold up Nicholas between them, relying on sound to stay in step with one another. The huge front door was still guarded and Esme didn't like Nicholas' chances of talking his way out, so Esme caused a distraction by throwing one shoe at one of the guards, then the other shoe at the other guard. Neither of them could have been particularly bright, because they started arguing with one another too fiercely to notice the Prince of the Kingdom of Mirrors hobbling past. Esme was vaguely aware of a kerfuffle amongst the guards further back in the building. Phrases like *can't touch the prisoners* and *why have all the circles turned red* floated out the door with them.

Outside it had begun to rain terribly, each drop the size of a pebble. Esme hoped it would aid their escape. Unfortunately, it also impeded their ability to see more than a couple of feet in front of them... and ruined Esme's socks. The waiting prisoners all must have noticed Prince Nicholas as he limped down the steps, but not one of them did more than blink, water dripping off their clothes into little puddles at their feet.

Esme wanted to cry.

She risked a glance behind her as they reached the bottom of the steps. She had no way of knowing if they were being followed—

'THE PRINCE HAS ESCAPED!' a voice screeched. Really, it shouldn't have taken them this long to notice.

'Come on!' she hissed. Nicholas was shuffling along like an elderly man, although the rain seemed to have revived him a little.

'There! You—stop—' a guard called to them, but Esme didn't turn around. She pulled Nicholas by the arm, eyes on the gate ahead. She could hear Violet rummaging in her pocket. A moment later Esme heard a popping sound, like a small firework had exploded, and an *oof* of breath as the guard collapsed. They were going to do it, they were going to make it—

Something swished through the air near Esme's ear.

She heard Violet crumple to the ground.

A moment later, Violet flickered back into visibility, holding her bangle. A slick wooden arrow protruded from her shoulder. Something red was oozing onto her sleeve. Esme abandoned Nicholas and dropped down into the sludge.

'Go!' Violet gasped. Her face was an unholy mess of bruises, her leg stuck awkwardly beneath her and her shoulder wound was smoking, the arrow sticking out at an odd angle. Esme clawed in her pockets for something—anything—to stop the bleeding.

'They'll kill you! I can help you up—'

'What did you find behind that door?' Violet interrupted. She couldn't see Esme but leaned toward the sound of her voice.

'A furnace.'

Violet winced.

'Esme, come on!' Nicholas looked on the verge of collapse, his helmet lost to the mud, but something of Amelia's countenance came over him. 'I'll make sure we come back for her, but we need to leave *now*!' Back in the castle, a bell was ringing.

Violet squinted in Esme's direction. Her skin was turning grey. 'I told you we needed a continuity plan.'

'They will *kill you*!'

'This arrow might be killing me anyway. I have all that protection magic. Trust me.'

Esme looked down at Violet and made herself focus on her face. 'I've got your dress back at home,' she said quietly. 'You can have it back as soon as we get you out of here.' She kissed Violet's cracked lips, told herself it was because it was the only part of her face that wasn't horrendously bruised, then scrambled to her feet and slid Violet's discarded bangle onto Nicholas' wrist, dragging him through the mud as fast as she could.

Behind them, Esme could hear Violet, buying them a few seconds. 'My name is Violet Beauchamp! My father is Alexandre Beauchamp! Do you really want to kill your boss's daughter? Help me stand up then—'

Something popped again, louder than before. Esme prayed Violet hadn't misjudged her aim.

The gates were shut, but she had a final potion from Prince George. She hurled a glass vial at the gate and it detonated, leaving a hole large enough for two people to wriggle through. Keeping a firm grip on Nicholas, she felt as though time slowed down. Their path was clear, but they didn't seem to get any closer. Esme counted her heartbeats and lost track within seconds. She could see their stagecoach, disguise abandoned, horses ready to go.

The moment they squirmed through the gate, she threw off her bangle, calling to Albertine, 'Go *now!*' Beside her, Nicholas spluttered back into visibility, looking even more like a corpse than two minutes ago.

Raphael threw the door open and jumped out, pulling them both into the carriage. Only then did Esme allow herself one last look back. She could barely see through the rain. A sea of guards flooded the courtyard, some on horseback. A few were chasing the coach, but most had been caught in the explosion from Violet's last potion. Was Violet amongst the bodies? Esme squinted. She was almost sure Violet had been dragged away, leaving nothing but indents in the sludge. Almost.

Esme opened the walnut.

Chapter Eight

Esme must have fallen asleep, because the next thing she knew, they were back on the Queen's Road. Nicholas was asleep opposite her, but Raphael nodded when she sat up. Someone had put a clean pair of socks and some boots next to her feet. 'We're at your parents' inn. They need to come with us.' He looked at her closely. 'Are you all right?'

'No. Come in and meet my parents.'

Carmel's Inn looked exactly the same as it had when she left: windows cheery and bright with candlelight, Bertie at the bar, Katerina at the reception desk. Carmel and Thomas took in the sight of Nicholas and Raphael with the practised disinterest of hospitality professionals.

'Where is Violet?' Carmel asked. 'Her parents came back here, you know, looking for her. They genuinely didn't realise she wasn't with them until they reached Margaret's castle. We said she'd gone to find them in Stormhaven Town and they headed back up there.'

'She was taken.' Esme did not know how else to tell them. 'We're leaving now,' she added. Something in her face quelled any discussion.

Up in her bedroom, Esme stared about at her belongings. What would she miss and want in a week's time? What would she miss in a month, or a year? She wanted Violet's shrinking spell. She wanted Violet. She wanted to curl in a ball and sleep for a decade.

She took a deep breath and stuffed some clothes, her sewing kit and her favourite books into a case. Violet's dress was folded carefully and placed on top of everything else.

Half an hour later the Delacroix family was officially homeless. Their belongings were packed, their magic paraphernalia given to friends and neighbours who were either willing to smuggle it or wanted to use it. Bertie and Katerina had been handed all the cash from the safe and told to go home. Thomas went up to the attic and returned, panting, with several gold bars. The part of Esme that was still awake thought, 'Well, that explains where the smuggling money went.'

Her mother locked the entrance door and Carmel's Inn was officially closed, its lamps out for the first time in Esme's memory. Their guests had been sent on to other inns along the road, Madame Velazquez taking far too much interest in Albertine's coach as she went.

The border was more difficult to manage. For one thing, the number of travellers holding placards had increased. Some were singing or holding hands. Some were standing on boxes, calling to their fellow travellers. For another thing, by now Nicholas and Raphael—and probably Esme, now she thought about it—would be on every border guard's Most Wanted list. Esme dug in her pockets and found tiny dregs of disguise potion in the bottle. They rubbed it on their faces and changed a little, but really they needed someone who could cast a good distraction spell. Esme felt her knees tremble, even though she was sitting down.

At the crossing, Thomas offered Georgiana's father one of the gold bars.

'You don't have to give me any of that,' he said gently. 'I know you've been up to... something.' He took in Nicholas's emaciated state, which the magic had done nothing to hide, and Esme's ashen expression, which she thought would probably be fixed until she died. 'You're a lovely family. Is there time for you to say goodbye to Georgiana?'

'I don't think so,' Esme said, a lump in her throat. She remembered Georgiana's aunt. 'You should tell your sister to come through as soon as possible. Bring the entire family.'

Mr Garcia searched their faces. 'We'll do that,' he said eventually. 'Now hurry up and get going.'

Nobody spoke for the entire journey, and the carriage did not stop once. Esme thought of Violet's ingenious way to keep the horses going and swayed in her seat. She wasn't sure what day it was. Had they escaped the Skeleton Rooms yesterday, or the day before? What might Violet be doing now? Esme took a deep breath and willed herself to stay in one piece.

When they reached the White Palace at Laketown, Prince George was there to meet them. Standing outside the gate, he held a duffel bag filled with books and stood next to a stagecoach with fresh horses.

'We're going to Lumiere,' he said with no preamble. 'Queen Hazel had a dream and woke us up in the middle of the night to leave. I'm the only one left.' Although not enamoured by the prospect of more travelling, Esme was relieved to put more distance between herself and the Skeleton Rooms. The coach rattled along so efficiently that Esme wondered if she would ever get used to non-magical travel. Nobody said much, although her parents kept looking at her sideways.

The party arrived at Lumiere at dusk, tired and hungry. Esme had an urge to wander the streets counting all the colours she could see, then wander the beach and the olive groves and the entire kingdom until her eyes stopped being open. She wondered if this ear-ringing emptiness was how Violet felt after being hit.

Amelia met them at the gate. She hugged her brother and brother-in-law and sent them straight to the infirmary. She gauged in a second that Esme did not have the energy for words, so she just took her by the hand and walked the Delacroix family to the Great Hall.

Esme had never seen so many fancy people in one place. She was suddenly conscious of her dirty clothing, and of her parents' broad accents. The hall did not just hold the two High Councils: every aristocrat and their staff from here to Laketown seemed to have been standing around waiting for Esme's arrival. Within minutes, a hundred seats were filled, and cups of wine hastily poured for the newcomers.

Esme took it all in: Princess Amelia and her parents; Prince Richard and his. A woman sat between Queen Florence and Queen Hazel who could only be Lady Valentina Rathbone, Florence's sister. Prince George sat on Richard's other side, looking as comfortable as a mermaid in the desert. Esme sat next to him with her parents, while the remainder of the seats were taken up by lords and ladies. It occurred to Esme that no one knew who was in charge. It seemed to have occurred to Amelia, too, because after everyone had sat for a moment or two, she stood up.

'Thank you for coming,' she began. 'Look, we all know why we're here. We have all heard rumours of Queen Margaret persecuting magic users across Stormhaven. It's estimated that in the last two years, at least five thousand people have fled to the Valley or the Kingdom of Mirrors. Recently a couple of concerned Stormhaven citizens brought evidence to the court's attention and offered to infiltrate the Skeleton Rooms themselves for further information.

'Here is the evidence they've uncovered.' She nodded at Esme, who stepped forward with the little walnut.

Twenty minutes later, a shocked silence settled over the crowd. A couple of people excused themselves. Esme wished she hadn't forced herself to watch every projection, from that first episode in the kitchen at the inn to the last minutes at the Skeleton Rooms. She noticed a few of the audience glance at her as hologram Violet lay in the sludge, pity and curiosity splashed across their faces. She blinked and glared at the floor.

'Now we know what we're dealing with,' Amelia began, voice brittle, 'we need to decide how to act.'

'*How* to act?' A lord in a spectacularly overstated waistcoat sat forward in his chair. 'Your Majesty, why is it assumed that we must act?'

'Because—' Amelia was cut off by her mother's hand on her arm. 'No, you're right, Lord Donald,' she admitted. 'I suppose the first thing we should do is decide whether we *should* act.'

'How about we break for dinner?' Queen Hazel suggested, 'and vote on our return? I think we all need time to take in what we've seen.' Esme remembered Amelia's remark about conducting court business on an empty stomach and almost smiled.

Half an hour later, Esme and her parents had been given clean clothes and bedrooms each with a bathroom larger than most rooms at the inn. Someone had placed the bags Violet and Esme left at the White Palace in Laketown next to Esme's wardrobe.

Esme put Violet's case at the back of the wardrobe.

As she left to find the kitchen, Esme heard her parents arguing in their bedroom.

'We shouldn't have let her go,' Carmel was saying. Esme could picture her ringing her hands.

'How were we to know what would happen?' Thomas countered. 'Stormhaven is dangerous for people like Esme. I'm amazed she's lived this long without someone she knows being imprisoned. It was the will of the gods that *she* was never arrested.'

There was a moment's pause. 'Where are we going to live?' Thomas asked. 'What will we do? Our gold won't last forever. Esme needs schooling…'

'We'll have to appeal to the court for refuge. We can take jobs in an inn. We'll be fine.'

Regret slipped through the despair in Esme's stomach. She shouldn't have involved her parents in this. She shouldn't have involved Violet. Violet shouldn't have involved Violet.

They ate in the kitchen with Amelia's family. Raphael joined them, looking far less worried and a lot cleaner. According to the castle physician, Nicholas was suffering from general over-exertion and would make a full recovery. Amelia threatened to let the goats loose in the castle if he didn't get out of bed soon.

'Thank you, Esme, for rescuing our son.' Queen Hazel said without ceremony as they sat down.

Esme rubbed her eyes. 'I just did what you asked.'

'You didn't have to, though,' the queen said quietly. 'We will always be grateful to you.'

'Thank you. And thank you for the protection spell. It saved my life in the—in the furnace.' Esme knew she should probably curtsey or something, but it was taking every bit of her energy to chew properly. She wished she could taste the food, because King Emmanuel and Queen Hazel were wonderful hosts. 'There's more you should know.'

'More?' Emmanuel looked like he would rather not know.

'About the reason Violet wouldn't let me drag her out of the prison. She and I had a plan for if one of us got caught. Well, Violet had a plan. Queen Margaret will want to know how we got into the Skeleton Rooms. Especially since Violet's the daughter of a member of Margaret's court. We agreed that if we were taken, we'd use the walnut trick to learn as much as we could while we were being interrogated. And we'd use our magic to do as much damage to the court as possible.'

'What sort of damage?' Hazel asked.

'My magic is entirely in my head, but there's a lot you can do with people who are terrified of the second sight. Violet's magic is more physical, though. I know she studied a lot. I wouldn't be surprised if something in the Skeleton Rooms or Margaret's castle explodes or catches fire soon. All we need to do is use the tracking magic, and she'll lead us to a very inconvenienced Margaret. If she's not already—if she's not—'

'We'll find Violet,' Emmanuel told her. 'We'll bring her back.' He glanced at Amelia, who stood up from the table.

'George's tracking spells worked, but they were weak when you were up in the mountains. I'll go to our magicians and best soldiers now and tell them they're leaving at first light to find her. Don't start the meeting without me.'

'Perish the thought.' The king poured tea as Amelia swept from the room, and Esme realised with a jolt that she hadn't given a thought to the witch in the woods since the morning she left for Laketown. Someone should have warned her what was going on—Esme should have remembered to think of her. After all, they shared a name. Esmeralda. How could an old lady, even a magical one, hold her own somewhere like the Skeleton Rooms?

'You'll pay me one day.' Was that what she had said? Did the witch know they would meet again someday? Esme swallowed. A stone seemed to have settled in her throat. She sniffed and wiped her nose on a serviette.

Carmel scooted her chair along the table and enveloped Esme in a hug.

Back in the Great Hall, an uneasy mood had settled over the congregation. The lords and ladies had had time to think, and their reflections had not gone down as well as their dinner. Amelia hurried in last, flustered. 'The tracking magic's still active,' she murmured in Esme's ear before taking her seat. 'Some of our best people are leaving at dawn.' A tiny part of Esme unwound, just a little.

King Richard stood. 'Citizens of the Valley of Dreams, I want you to know that this will be a free discussion, and a free vote. Queen Florence and I cannot force you into action but I can tell you that if we choose not to take a stand against Stormhaven now, I believe we will be on the wrong side of history.'

Queen Hazel stood too. 'King Emmanuel, Princess Amelia and I feel the same. All in favour of taking direct action against Stormhaven in response to the crimes being carried out at the Skeleton Rooms?'

Every hand in the room went up.

'We are agreed, then.' Hazel looked around at the room. 'The next question is, what action?'

'We *start* with talks,' Lady Valentina suggested. 'I don't think they will work, but I want it on record that we did not simply declare war on our neighbour. The Three Kingdoms are not the old clans. We must conduct ourselves peacefully wherever possible. Why is Margaret committing this atrocity? What made her decide to fund a plot to kidnap Prince Richard last year?'

'I think she's playing a long game,' Prince George said quietly. He was holding Violet's diary. He looked around the room. 'I'm the only person here who knows Margaret's court. It's like a spider's web. Violet Beauchamp recorded evidence that at least four of my uncles and cousins are involved with the Skeleton Rooms, and that a couple of aunts were involved with the Eaton Plot. You can guarantee Margaret knows about all of it and encouraged where she saw fit. She hasn't officially named her successor,' he added, in response to confused looks. 'Her children and siblings have been at each other's throats for decades, all trying to gain her favour. No one is more aware of that than Margaret herself. She sees everyone as a threat. She could be using fear of magic users to stir her court into a frenzy... maybe ordering something as horrible as what's happening in the Skeleton Rooms would weed out the weak members of her court and prove who's worthy of following her onto the throne.

Maybe she wants to watch the family rip itself to shreds. Or both,' he added after a moment's thought.

'But genocide?' King Richard asked. 'Would she go that far just to decide who's worthy of the crown?'

George shrugged. 'She really, really hates magic users. I think she's been looking for an excuse to get rid of us for years.'

'That doesn't explain why she's causing dissent in the other two kingdoms,' Queen Hazel argued.

'It does,' pointed out King Emmanuel, 'when you consider that if we were distracted by something like a hostage situation with one of our children and blaming one another, she could probably get on with her schemes without anyone noticing. Think about it... if Prince Richard hadn't seen through Alistaire Eaton's kidnap attempt, and Miss Delacroix hadn't had a vision of the Skeleton Rooms and come to us, we would be none the wiser to any of this.' *There was the notebook*, Esme thought. *Violet noticed everything.*

'I still feel we're missing something,' Queen Hazel pressed. 'Miss Delacroix and her family told us about the unrest at the border crossing on the Queen's Road. If news of what's really going on at the Skeleton Rooms broke to the people of Stormhaven, I imagine they would do a lot more than protest with some placards. Could Queen Margaret be trying to stir her people into a civil war? But then, to what end? What if—'

A door clanged open. 'Pardon me, Your Majesties,' a guard looked terrified to have interrupted such an important meeting, but he swallowed and strode to the monarchs at the top of the room. 'Excuse me for interrupting, it's just—we've just had word—Queen Margaret's army has just invaded the northern border of the Valley of Dreams. It seems there's quite a lot of them, Your Majesties, and they're quite well armed.'

'Well, then.' Amelia broke the silence. 'It looks like that's what we were missing.'

Epilogue

Each of the royal families of the Three Kingdoms ascended their throne via either a war or a marriage. This is also how they came to fall from their thrones. You can still find valiant young men, although they're less witty than they once were, and you can still find silver-tongued elderly ladies, although they're rarer than they once were.

The health and safety standards, it must be said, have plummeted.

Read on for bonus *Three Kingdoms* stories

The Kingdom Mirror
Tuesday, 12th September

Princess Amelia's First Solo Royal Engagement Marred by Accident

Mixed success for Crown Princess Amelia's first solo royal engagement

By Royal Correspondent Nicholas Snitchell

Princess Amelia has completed her first solo royal engagement, albeit not as successfully as one may have hoped. The thirteen-year-old, who was officially proclaimed crown princess in August, following her brother Prince Nicholas' shock abdication in March, has until yesterday undertaken engagements with her parents, King Emmanuel and Queen Hazel, or her brother. Princess Amelia spent Monday morning at the Lumiere Hospital for Veterans of War, meeting children of injured service people, followed by lunch with staff. She spent the afternoon with patients in the hospital's recently refurbished rehabilitation facility.

The Princess was her trademark friendly, inquisitive self, enthusiastically joining children in their arts and crafts projects, and taking a great interest in the logistics of rehabilitation and treatment. Her table manners were noted by staff as exemplary and the engagement considered a roaring success until late afternoon, when Princess Amelia leant on a magic pully system elevating a soldier's injured leg. The system collapsed, its residual force severing the newly reattached leg from its owner. Emergency surgery was required, but doctors were able to re-reattach the leg and are confident of a full recovery. The soldier, who wished not to be named publicly, will need months more specialist treatment at a time when hospitals are nearing capacity thanks to recent assaults by the Sapphire Dragon.

Irini Marchetti, chief correspondent of *Royal Watch*, this paper's entertainment magazine, sums up the princess's first engagement: 'Princess Amelia made a gallant effort, but she's just not as well loved as her parents the King and Queen or her older brother, Prince Nicholas. It may take years to persuade people of the Kingdom of Mirrors that she's a worthy successor to her father and older brother, especially if every event proves as calamitous as this one!'

Liliane di Antonio, a soldier having treatment at the Lumiere Hospital for Veterans of War, told us: 'I think the Princess did a fantastic job. How many thirteen-year-olds are having lunch with leading medical staff? That pully system was ridiculous anyway. Is that enough gossip or would you like me to fabricate some?'

Royal Watch Magazine
Thursday 28th February

The Ascension of Amelia

In her first ever interview, Crown Princess Amelia, 13, talks to chief correspondent Irini Marchetti of Royal Watch magazine about royal life and adjusting to her increasing responsibilities.

Your Majesty, thank you for taking the time out of your busy schedule to talk to the kingdom's number one entertainment magazine! How are you following the recent turmoil?
Well, the latest assault by the Sapphire Dragon is terrible for the kingdom's farmers and means that another chunk of the Kingdom of Mirrors will be inhospitable for the foreseeable future. I'm devastated for everyone who's lost their home or livelihood. But we're working with the witches in the eastern groves to help nature recover as soon as possible. We've permanently re-housed all the refugees, and they're settling into their new homes very well given the circumstances.

That's a very sage answer from someone so young! I was actually talking about the stroke suffered by your father, King Emmanuel, in September. It must have been devastating for you!
Oh, right. Thank you for asking. I'm fine. When it first happened it was a shock, as he's always been very healthy. It's hard, you know, to watch someone when they're ill. But the nursing staff are fantastic. He's already talking about returning to some duties.

How do you feel about that?
I feel that if the king says he can do something, there's not a lot we can do about it…

It's been six months since you assumed the role of Crown Princess. Some of your actions and decisions have raised eyebrows across the kingdoms! How are you finding your new responsibilities?
They're… challenging but enjoyable. I spend most of my time in the Treasury now, or with the High Council. I haven't been to school since my father's stroke, as there is so much to do with the war and everything. But I would have to assume all my father's duties eventually anyway.

Have you heard from your brother, Prince Nicholas, recently? The royal wedding must be soon. Is there any truth to the rumours that the wedding will be a completely private event?
I had a suspicion you might ask about the wedding, so I wrote to Nicholas and asked what they're planning. I have his response here, bear with me… 'Tell Marchetti that we think there might be a bit of resistance to a taxpayer-funded booze up for hundreds of our closest friends and aristocrats, given that half the kingdom thinks I should be flayed alive for abdicating. Tell her we're getting married in a pigsty, where Raphael belongs.' You did write that in your column, didn't you?

Well, yes, but I'm only saying what people are thinking. Does Nicholas have any regrets about abdicating?
Oh, I have that here, too. 'If Marchetti wants a sob story about how much I regret throwing my life away, tell her I recently skinned a goat, and that the smell reminded me of her journalism.'

Er, right. Now, are there any boys in your life at the moment?
Um, I spent most of the time in the Treasury. I'm also thirteen?

Your brother was just eighteen when he abdicated…
Before I left school, my health and citizenship class did a whole term about relationships, so I know for a fact that eighteen is probably old enough to decide who you're going to marry, but that thirteen definitely isn't. My tutor Madame Louisa says that magazines like *Royal Watch* cater to a depressing cultural attitude in which young women are only valuable once we're… actually, I can't tell you exactly what she said. She was having quite a rant at the time. But I'm starting to think she has a point.

Right… There are rumours that your parents could arrange a marriage for you and take that decision right out of your hands! Do you think that's any different to your brother's situation?

My brother abdicated so he *didn't* have to go through with an arranged marriage. And those rumours are about as credible as the ones saying Queen Margaret locked one of her nephews in a tower.

Well, that's us told! Finally: what sort of queen do you hope to be?

One who ascends the throne when she is very old.

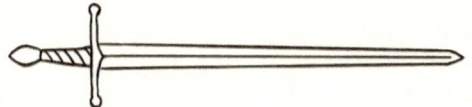

The Queen of Stormhaven

They all turned out for her coronation. Every lord, lady and peasant. Some brought their children, others their dogs. All wearing the colours of the light gods: saffron, scarlet, pomegranate. Their happiest finery, for the happiest of days. Many tied prayer flags to the trees lining the route of her celebratory parade. Luck, health and prosperity for the Three Kingdoms' youngest ever monarch. Eight years and eight weeks old on her coronation day, beating the previous record by over a decade.

'I feel the gods are with you,' smiled the priest when he ran her through her responsibilities for the coronation ceremony. 'I sense you will rule for a very long time, Your Majesty, over a prosperous kingdom. The gods have blessed you with a strong heart and a steady head.'

'They blessed my mother with the same thing,' she replied, and the smile faltered a tiny bit.

Seven years and sixteen weeks: the age at which Margaret de Winter inherited the Stormhaven throne. Seven years and seventeen weeks: the age at which she led her mother's funeral procession along the same route her coronation parade took. The same crowd turned out for both: blue and black for one occasion, rainbow hues for the next. She even spotted the same faces in the same foldable chairs.

How many had prayed for her mother's good health on *her* coronation day? How many prayed when the screaming fever crept through the castle windows and into Queen Alexandria's brain?

One of the high priests, the one who anointed Margaret in the holiest part of the coronation ceremony, had been one of Alexandria's physicians. He'd prescribed everything: calming salves, sleeping potions, enchanted water, herbs grown in the Kingdom of Mirrors by the witches of the eastern groves. He was the first to realise that it wasn't just screaming fever that was eating the queen from the inside out.

'It's all the magic,' he explained to Margaret and her father, the prince consort. 'Queen Alexandria is an accomplished magician, Your Majesties.

One of the very finest to study at the Valley University of Spells and Enchantments. Her work during the Great Storm of Saturnalia kept half of Stormhaven from falling into the Eastern Ocean. And I've never seen anyone conjure light so fast! But it's taken its toll on her constitution, I'm afraid. She simply hasn't got the strength to fight a screaming fever of this magnitude.'

'What can I do?' Margaret asked.

'Pray, Your Majesty. Her life is in the hands of the gods now.'

Eight years and nine weeks: the age at which Queen Margaret de Winter issued her first law, criminalising the teaching of magic in public spaces. Eight years and ten weeks: the age she shut all temples with immediate effect. Nine years and one week: the age by which all practise of magic and/or worship had been completely banned in Stormhaven.

The priest had been right, though: she ruled for a very, very long time.

Acknowledgements

Endless Sapphire Dragon soft toys to the dragonnovel dream team: Ruby, Ellen, Ryan, Tatchiana, Robyn, Sarah and Isobel. Potions galore to Maria em-dash Solecki. Eternal fuss for the world's least interested sounding boards, Fred you've-forgotten-to-feed-me and Adonis can-I-sit-on-your-keyboard Burke.

No. 1 Readers' Club Thank Yous

Ely, Grant, Sarah, Ellen, Melody, Maria, Sonia Marie, Sarah, Natalie. Join the No. 1 Readers' Club at https://patreon.com/FrancescasWords.

About the Author

Born in Rochford in 1995, Francesca Astraea decided at an early age that the worlds inside books and television were infinitely preferable to the real one. Initially put off the idea of being a writer because it requires one to sit alone and ignore people, she now finds sitting alone and ignoring people to be the most satisfying parts of the job. She lives in Southend-on-Sea.

Learn more about Francesca at https://francescaswords.com.